Kelly's Fancy

by

Owen Kelly

GREYSTONE BOOKS
1991

First published by Greystone Books Ltd, 1991.

ISBN 1 870157 13 3

Cover: Leslie Stannage Design.
Printed by W. & G. Baird Ltd at the Greystone Press, Antrim.

Contents

1 *The Hafner's Sausages*

The Hafner's sausages saga began one Friday night in the pub. I just happened to mention that I was going to Dublin the next day and Paddy, who claims to have more things to do on a Saturday than an ordinary fellow would line up for a week, announced that he would come with me. That way he could put off until the following weekend the things he should have done the weekend before.

Up till that moment Jim had been staring morosely into his pint. He came to life with a great start.

'Dublin,' he said wistfully. 'I wish I could go with you.'

'Ah, come on with us,' I said. 'The journey will be all the shorter with the three of us driving.'

'I can't,' Jim said glumly. 'The wife's people are coming up from Tyrone tomorrow for the day's shopping. It would look bad if I wasn't there.'

'That's true,' Paddy agreed. 'It would look as if you didn't want to have anything to do with them.'

'I don't,' Jim said, as gloomy as ever, 'but I don't want them to know that I don't want to know, if you see what I mean.'

'It's a question of diplomacy,' I remarked. 'Say no more.'

'Hafner's sausages,' said Jim, back to staring gloomily into his glass.

'That's what's called a non sequitur,' I told Paddy.

'The taxpayers of this country got a bargain when they paid for your schooling,' Paddy observed. 'What's a non whatever you said?'

'Hafner's sausages,' I explained, 'have nothing whatever to do with Jim's in-laws, or out-laws, coming up from Tyrone tomorrow for the shopping. Ergo, a non sequitur.'

'I don't know a single work of Foreign,' was his response. 'What are Hafner's sausages and how did they get into this conversation anyway?'

'Funny you should say that,' I said. 'What class of a sausage is a Hafner anyway?'

Jim took his eyes off his pint and looked at us with the air of a botanist who has just discovered a new and dubious specimen.

'First of all,' he said, 'Hafner's sausages are not a non sequitur. They have everything to do with the in-laws. If they weren't coming up from Tyrone for the shopping tomorrow I'd go down to Dublin with you two and buy a serious amount of them. Second of all, Hafner's sausages are the finest food known to the human palate, and every time I hear Dublin mentioned I get a terrible craving for them. You can only get them in Dublin.'

'Tell me something,' I said, 'in what way do they differ from what your man across the road sells?'

He gave me a withering look.

'Wait till I tell you,' he informed me, 'It's like what Louis Armstrong said about jazz. Some half-eejit asked him what jazz was and Ol' Satchmo said, "Son, if you gotta ask, you'll never get to know".'

'I'm a meat and two veg man myself,' I apologised. 'You make these things sound like a deeply moving spiritual experience. It's probably because of my unsophisticated palate that I've never heard of these delicacies. My apologies.'

'Noted,' said Jim. 'Of course, it's years since I ate a plateful of Hafner's sausages, so you'll understand why I get a bit lyrical on the subject.'

'How many years?' Paddy asked.

'Twenty,' said Jim and his eyes misted over.

Paddy looked at me and I looked at him. Twenty years is a very long time to be deprived of anything.

'There was a man in a story one time,' I remarked, 'and when he made his fortune in America he came back to Ireland looking for pancakes the way his old mother used to make them. He offered prizes. Pancake makers came from all over the land and they baked away like mad but none of them could produce the goods. Nobody could make pancakes the way his old mother could when he was a boy.'

The other two gave me a very odd look.

'What is your point, exactly?' Paddy asked.

'Simple,' I said. 'Your man hadn't the taste buds he had when his old mother was making the pancakes.'

'You have no soul,' Paddy told me. 'Tell us, Jim, why did you suddenly decide you wanted Hafner's sausages, apart from hearing Dublin mentioned? Are you suffering, maybe, from some biological queerness? Are you sympathetically pregnant, perhaps?'

'No, nothing like that,' Jim assured us. 'I lust after Hafner's sausages all the time. It just gets worse when Dublin comes up in conversation, that's all.'

'But surely,' I said, 'you must have been in Dublin dozens of times in the last twenty years?'

'Only to matches,' he told me sadly. 'And when you don't drive, and you're dependent on other people, and by the time you get out of the pub and one thing or another, you don't get all that many butchers' shops open at that hour of the night.'

'True enough,' said Paddy sympathetically, 'but say no more. Come what may, tomorrow you shall have your heart's desire. You shall have Hafner's sausages up to the armpits. Consider it done.'

'A couple of pounds would do,' said Jim. 'Just enough to taste my mouth.'

'Whatever,' Paddy assured him, turning his glass upside down in a pointed manner. 'Your shout, I believe.'

I called for Paddy the next morning at eleven, and found him reading the paper and working his way through a mountain of toast. He still had to shave, find his socks and make several phone calls. I mentioned the time factor. He said Dublin had been in the same place for a thousand years and would probably still be there whatever time we arrived. I had a meeting at four o'clock but prudently lied and told him it was at two. That way we might make it for three.

'Let us not forget the Hafner's sausages,' he solemnly intoned as we finally turned on to the motorway. 'Above all, let us not forget that.'

We drove along, chatting idly of this and that, possibly other topics as well, when he suddenly asked me if I'd seen the previous night's paper.

'There was a photograph of a dog in it,' he said. 'You've never seen the like of it. It's a special breed. It can fit into a pint glass. There's a man in Banbridge breeds them. He has a pub.'

'Don't tell me,' I said. 'We're going to detour via Banbridge to see these pint-sized dogs.'

'It would add to the sum of our experience,' he replied.

We found the pub in Banbridge but we could hardly walk in and ask to see the dogs, just like that. Paddy had a pint and I, relegated to driving for the day, dallied with a glass of orange. We talked to the barman about the weather in such profound tones you'd have thought we had some control over it.

Paddy mentioned the dogs. Ah, well, you see, the owner kept them out at his mother's place and he was out there now, bringing one in for a customer. He'd be back in five minutes, ten at the most. Paddy had another pint, I consumed a reluctant orange, we put the finishing touches to the weather report but an hour later the publican hadn't come back so we deferred the dog experience to a later time and resumed the trek to Dublin.

We made it as far as Dundalk before Paddy announced that the beneficial effects of the mountain of toast had worn off and not a yard farther would we go until he had something to eat. He was acquainted with the lady in charge of a well-known restaurant, though how and why this was so I never enquired. She asked him what had brought him down that way.

'We're on a pilgrimage,' he said. 'We're in search of Hafner's sausages for a sick friend. They have miraculous properties.'

It was near enough four o'clock when I dropped him off at Drumcondra, where he announced that he would do two things. He would visit his sister and he would, without fail, come what may, acquire two pounds of Hafner's sausages. He further undertook to meet me in the Green Goose at seven o'clock on the dot.

He was indeed in the Green Goose when I got back from my meeting at seven. He and several citizens of Dublin were at the blood brother stage and had been sorting out the world situation at an astonishing rate. Over every convivial gathering, however, a tiny cloud must cast its shadow. In this case the shadow was substantial, sober and anxious to be on the way home. I waited for a spontaneous lull in the conversation before stepping up behind his chair.

'Hafner's sausages,' I said.

He looked blankly round at me. So did the rest of the gathering.

'Begod,' he announced, with a look of amazement, 'You'll never believe this. I forgot all about the bloody sausages.'

He turned to the blood brothers.

'Where could a fella get a couple of pounds of Hafner's sausages at this time of the night?' he implored them earnestly.

You wouldn't have though that a simple thing like sausages could generate so much controversy. One man informed us, in tones that invited no contradiction, that they could only be got in Hafner's shop in the city centre and it was shut. Another authoritative voice announced that it had been shut for twenty years. Not at all, somebody else said, it was a brand name now, you could ask in any butcher's shop for them. But, another expert broke in, it's after seven, even butchers had homes to go to on a Saturday night. Various people thought this unreasonable, in view of the emergency situation. Nobody present had ever tasted the sausages, though they quoted extensively from parents, even grandparents. Personal experience was thin on the ground.

I reminded Paddy that he had only one tiny thing to remember and he couldn't manage that much. He said, sure anybody could make a mistake, and what about the old sausages anyway, it was only a notion of Jim's, nothing more, he'd probably forgotten all about them by now. This was the optimism of the slightly intoxicated, and I deflated it with a reference to Jim's need for uplift after a day's exposure to the in-laws. Paddy relented.

'You're right,' he said. 'We'd better go and look for the sausages after all.'

There are several disadvantages in going to look for sausages after eight o'clock on a Saturday night on the north side of Dublin, especially if you're looking for a brand name and more especially if the few corner shops still open have never heard of the brand. I began to think Jim had plotted the whole thing to spoil our day because his was ruined, too.

At our last effort, a mini-market on the way to the airport, we explained our problem to the owner. He was manning the cash register and he listened with the indulgent sneer of the professional for amateurs. He had heard of Hafner's sausages. From his mother. We could take his word for it. No such thing was available.

'We can't go back and tell Jim that,' I said. 'He'll think we just forgot and we're making excuses.'

'The memory,' the shopkeeper said, 'is a chancy thing. Now, I have the best of sausages here. If your man can tell the difference between them and Hafner's, he's a better man than all three of us put together.'

He took a packet of a well-known brand from the freezer. It was cellophane-wrapped, thick with ice and and wouldn't have fooled a five-year-old. I mentioned this point. The shopkeeper smiled a knowing smile.

'What we'll do is this,' he said. 'We'll open four of these half pound packets and wrap the sausages in brown paper and string. I'll bet you the price of them your friend couldn't remember the shape and size of those Hafner's to save his life. When you get back to Belfast you'll have a damp, two pound pack of sausages, just like in the old times and your man will be none the wiser.'

I told the shopkeeper he would have done well in my own home town in south Derry and he dismembered the cellophane packs, parcelled the lot up without even an extra penny for either his trouble or his professional expertise.

Things might have ended differently if we'd gone straight home at this point, but a fine singsong in a roadside pub drew Paddy like a magnet. He could afford to be indulgent because I was driving but the crack was good in spite of the orange juice. It was well into Sunday morning before we trundled across the border and into the stern rectitude of an Ulster Sabbath.

Paddy was sound asleep when we arrived at Jim's gate, so indeed was the whole world, except for me, but the ding-dong of Jim's door chimes wakened the dogs in the houses on either side. They in turn wakened Jim. He put his cross head out of the bedroom window and enquired who the hell was there.

'Hafner's sausages,' I called up and it wasn't true on any count.

Within seconds he was at the door informing me that I was a prince among men, a tribute he repeated when I told him to consider the sausages a gift. He even assumed an air of spurious regret when I declined, on behalf of the sleeping Paddy and myself, his invitation to come in while he fried some of them for the three of us.

I emptied Paddy out of the passenger seat at his front door, vowed never to take him anywhere again and went home. The sky was lightening in the east, where the wise men supposedly came from, when I sidestepped the creaky board on our stairs and slipped gratefully into bed.

The following Friday night Paddy and I were in our accustomed places in the pub when Jim rambled in, exuding peace and good fellowship. We had agreed not to mention sausages in his presence.

'What sort of crack did you have with the in-laws?' Paddy asked, for he has a way of rushing in where angels wouldn't go without an armed escort. Jim snorted.

'They'd drive you to drink if you were a teetotaller,' he said, 'The only thing was, I had the Hafner's sausages to look forward to. Mind you,' he went on, looking at us both in an alarming way, 'I had doubts about that, too.'

'What sort of doubts?' Paddy demanded.

'Well, I never thought you two would remember,' Jim said. 'I know you two on a day out. Sure half the time you couldn't remember your own names if somebody asked you suddenly.'

'I resent that,' I told him. 'I don't deny it but I resent it.'

'Well, what about the sausages?' Paddy enquired, suddenly reckless.

'Wait till I tell you,' he said. And we waited.

'I fried the whole lot, first thing on Sunday morning.' He told us. 'There wasn't one left in half an hour.'

'Gluttony,' said Paddy piously. 'There's no other word for it.'

'Ah, now, hold on a minute,' Jim protested 'There was the wife, and the three youngsters and a couple of in-laws from Tyrone that stayed the night, all for breakfast. If I got half a dozen, it was the height of it. I'll tell you this, though. Quality tells. Nothing has changed. They tasted just the way I remember them. Wonderful.'

'Tell me something,' said Paddy as he dropped me off later that night. 'Who wrote the story about the pancakes?'

'A decent, scholarly but now deceased man from Donegal,' I told him, 'a first class storyteller.'

'And maybe he was, too,' was Paddy's parting remark, 'and maybe he was sound on pancakes. But I think he wouldn't have had a clue about sausages.'

2 *The Brorn Law*

Of course you've heard of the Brorn Law. There's no escaping his legend. He's all-wise, all-seeing, all-knowing. He's been everywhere and done everything. Your Man is his greatest fan. The Brorn Law is married to Your Man's sister. They form, jointly, the Brorn Law's fan club.

There are no flies on the Brorn Law. He knows what's going on in high places, and in low ones, too. There's no subject on which he's not expert, with the possible exception of the Theory of Relativity, and in that case he knows the man who knows all about it. Sure they were at school together. They're like that. The first and second fingers are held up, clamped tightly together to preclude any possibility of misunderstanding. He never makes a move without consulting the Brorn Law.

Of course, you understand that the Brorn Law takes no lip from anybody. Any petty bureaucrat who attempts to thwart him in the exercise of his rights can expect a sharp lesson in the facts of life. If he can't get satisfaction at local level, he'll go all the way to the top. Even to Stormont. In extreme cases, to Stormount. He knows the head man. Knew him when he had no backside to his trousers. There is no closer kinship, no more powerful clout.

You meddle with the Brorn Law at your peril.

He's a genius with his hands. He can do anything, no problem. Did Your Man never tell you about the time he bought the clapped-out foreign jalopy – they're not made any more, you know – in a scrapyard for twenty quid. No, he tells a lie, it was a tenner, or was it fifteen, anyway, it doesn't matter, he put it through the MOT for another tenner.

Rebuilt the whole works. Wait till Your Man tells you, he was out in that yard till all hours, but it was worth it, you should have seen it, he re-upholstered the seats and all. Worth it? Don't talk to Your Man about worth it. Thing turned out to be a collector's item. Brorn Law sold it to a collector for five hundred.

Now, of course, you understand he could have had a grand for it, no problem, but there was one wee snag. There was one part that couldn't be got, high up or low down, so he had to make one himself. From a bit of an old washing machine, naturally.

It had to be modified but that was no problem. Did the job himself on The Cousin's lathe. Fitted like a glove, worked like a clock, probably outlast the motor. Of course he had to tell the buyer it wasn't the original, just in case. Hence the huge drop in the asking price. Dead straight, the Brorn Law.

Fitted his own kitchen, plumbing, wiring the lot. You want to see what those cowboys were going to charge The Sister. Now The Sister, known to the Brorn Law as Namea God Woman, Ah, sure God love her, she hasn't a clue about prices. Those chancers – a long-established and reputable concern to all but the Brorn Law – were talking telephone numbers. Well, he soon put a stop to that. You want a new kitchen, says he, you'll get a new kitchen.

Well, of course, he had the job done in no time. He had all the tools and naturally he knew a fella that could get him all the stuff wholesale. OK, maybe a bit less than wholesale, but it's all above board, nothing off the back of a lorry or anything like that. The Brorn Law wouldn't touch anything dodgy, no way. The constabulary aren't going to turn up on his doorstep asking questions about bent gear.

Well, the whole operation only cost a quarter of what those cowboys were charging. The Brorn Law says, you take a basic thing like brackets, they're a rip-off. See those new, machined, snap-together jobs? Wouldn't have them about the place, you're just paying for the name and the fancy wrapping, that's all. What's wrong with good old-fashioned three inch steel brackets and a good screwdriver, that's what he wants to know. Last a lifetime.

And another thing. Pay three quid a time for adjustable hinges? You gotta be joking. You can't beat the good old book hinge, that's what the Brorn Law says. You could swing your whole weight on a cupboard door hung with good old steel hinges. You just try that with your fancy adjustable hinges and see what happens.

There is no healthier or fitter specimen on the surface of the planet than the Brorn Law. Doctors? Don't talk to Your Man about doctors. Brorn Law never went near a doctor in his life, smokes forty a day and enjoys a pint or three. Moderation in all things, that's his motto. Well, now, he did have a wee touch of rheumatism the year before last but he soon sorted that out with a drop of stuff he got from an old fella up in Ballybeyond.

No, you do not rub this stuff into the affected part. You drink it. No, it is not, definitely not, poteen, there's no way the Brorn Law would touch anything the full quota of excise duty had not been paid on. You'd never know what might be in it, you see.

No, this was a different class of stuff entirely, made by boiling the bark of a tree. Sorry, lips are sealed, the name and species of tree cannot be mentioned. The Brorn Law promised the old fella up in Ballybeyond that he would keep his secret. What you do is add two spoonfuls of Glauber salts to the brew, take a half'un of this prescription every morning on an empty stomach. Right as rain in a week.

It is not advisable to question the wisdom of putting this obnoxious concoction into the human inside. The Brorn Law, like God, is not mocked, not in the presence of his disciple anyway.

You must appreciate that a lot of people would give a fortune to get their hands on the formula but the old fella in Ballybeyond has always refused to part with it. In fact the only reason he took the Brorn Law into his confidence was that his father and the Brorn Law's father once paddled a canoe together to the head waters of the Amazon. The Brorn Law's acquaintances among ordinary mortals is strictly limited. Namea God Woman and Your Man, her brother, are about the lot.

Do not, if you value your peace of mind, ever mention any item of expenditure to Your Man. This is particularly important if it was a major investment. Why didn't you say something, sure he could have got the Brorn Law to organise it for you for less than half the price.

He knows the manager of that place well. Didn't he get him the job? Did Your Man never tell you about that? Funny, he thought he did. Well, you see, the guy before him had his fingers in the till and nobody knew anything about it till the Brorn Law saw him flashing the wads of fivers at Down Royal races and put two and two together. Lost the lot and not a bother on him. He's not playing with his own money, says the Brorn Law to himself, and tipped the wink to the boss on the golf course the next day.

Well, the boss was grateful. Any time you want anything, or any of your friends, just give me a buzz, I'll see you right, that's what he told the Brorn Law.

I actually met the Brorn Law once. Your Man introduced us, but the moment was ill-chosen, for he appeared to be in the grip of a great sorrow that afternoon. The racing page had fallen from his listless grasp and the forest of empty glasses on the table spoke of sorrows being drowned. Your Man, the disciple, smote him on the shoulder.

'What about ye, oul' han'?' he said jovially. 'How are things in Glockamorra?'

The Brorn Law focused on us with some difficulty.

'Sod 'em in Glockamorra,' he said, and his eyes went out of focus again.

That's another thing about the Brorn Law. He's a fierce man for the repartee.

3 *Crossed Lines*

It seems to me I never get a worthwhile crossed line these days. Time was I dialled a number and never knew what novel, enriching experience might be mine for the listening to.

I once nearly got a new shirt through the medium of a crossed line. I'd dialled somewhere or other and found myself in the midst of a conversation in which He figured prominently. He, by the way, wasn't the Almighty, just the husband of one half of the conversation.

I gently replaced the receiver and allowed a decent interval to elapse before trying my number again. The same electronic gremlins led me back into the middle of the same character assassination.

'And that's another thing,' said one voice. 'He wouldn't wear the shirt. It's still in the box. He just took one look at it and said take that (expletive deleted) thing back, I wouldn't be caught dead in that (same colourful expletive deleted again) object.'

'And what did you do?' asked the other voice.

'Well, nothing,' the first voice answered. 'I think maybe I'll give it to the bazaar. You don't like to bring things back.'

Female reluctance to bring things back to shops was a revelation to me.

'What size is it?' I asked. All right, it was wrong, I shouldn't have done it but I did.

'It's a sixteen collar, pale blue,' said the purchaser of the unwanted garment. 'Here, who the hell are you?'

Voice number two weighed in at this point with some advice for voice number one to pass on to me. The language of some people is really shocking. I'm sure there's some sort of law against saying that sort of thing on the phone.

I was only trying to emulate the success of a friend of mine who found himself in a similar conversation, except that the subject was the dietary value of baked beans. One of the voices had apparently just put some on the heat.

'Missus,' he said, 'I can smell your beans burning.'

He was rewarded with a scream, an invocation to the Holy Family and the line to himself.

The adventure of the wrong number has replaced the crossed line and its moment of high drama and low farce. I rang a restaurant in Magherafelt one night and asked if the proprietor was in.

'Noo,' said a slow, thoughtful voice. An expensive silence followed. I asked when he would be in.

'What number were you wanting?' the slow, thoughtful voice queried. I recited the Magherafelt number, complete with code, and the slow, thoughtful voice broke into a slow, thoughtful laugh.

'Och, no,' said the owner of the voice. 'You've got a wrong number. This is the island of Barra.'

I apologised at speed, for in my mind's eye I could see the wheels that counted my bill whirling like dervishes.

'Och, don't bother apologising,' said the slow, thoughtful voice. 'We don't get all that many calls here.'

Thanks to the mixed blessings of modern technology I got to pass the time of day with an invisible crofter in the Western Isles. Och aye.

I've been on the receiving end of many a wrong number and it's a mixed blessing. I rarely rush to answer the phone because no matter what the poet said about the bell tolling, it rarely tolls for me. This is one of the peculiar advantages of being outnumbered by daughters. When the phone did ring persistently early one Monday morning, I ignored it and continued shaving, secure in the knowledge that it couldn't possibly be for me. Then it dawned on me that I had the house to myself and that it was my sacred duty to fulfil my role as message-taker. So I uttered the selection of imprecations that I kept handy for these occasions and abandoned the shaving operation.

'Is that you?' a female voice enquired.

I studied my reflection, pinkish on one side and foam-covered on the other like a half-finished Santa Claus and was satisfied with the identity check.

'Yes,' I replied truthfully.

'Do you know who this is?' the caller enquired.

As a general thing there's nothing I like better than standing around half-shaved on a Monday morning, playing guessing games with a coy, disembodied and possibly deranged stranger.

'No,' I said tersely.

'Ah, go on, have a guess,' the voice went on. See what I mean? Crazy.

'You are Margaret Thatcher, formerly Prime Minister over beyond, and I claim the prize,' I told my invisible inquisitor.

'Oh, aye, this is Maggie all right,' the caller informed me, 'but not that one. I wish I had her money, that's all.'

Of all the names in the calendar of saints I had to pick the right one. Somebody up there didn't like me too much that morning.

'You're looking well, Maggie,' I ventured.

'Here, how do you know?' she demanded.

'I have a particular insight into these matters,' I informed her. 'I have a cousin who is the seventh son of a seventh son, twice removed.'

The shaving lather was setting like cement, giving out little crackling sounds of warning as it became part of the skin. Regret was setting in, too. I had made a fundamental error. You should only keep people talking to prevent them from jumping off a high building. Maggie seemed comfortable.

'How are you keeping yourself?' she asked solicitously. 'Are you all right?'

'Great,' I assured her. 'If I was any better I couldn't stick it.'

'That's good,' she said. "What are you doing for pastime these days anyway?'

'Oh, training, as usual,' I informed her.

'That's all you hear these days,' she said. 'Training and dieting. That won't make you any younger, you know. What are you training for anyway?'

'The Olympics,' I told her. 'I've a chance of a place on the Irish formation dancing team.'

I could sense a deterioration in our relationship at this point.

'Here,' she said, a bit crossly, 'you're pulling my leg.'

'I would not,' I assured her, 'dream of touching your leg.'

'Listen,' she snapped, all business, 'Can I speak to Harry?'

'There's no Harry here,' I broke the news gently.

The disembodied Maggie's voice rose a decibel or two.

'What number is that?' she squeaked.

'What number were you calling?' I enquired cautiously. She told me. I told her I wasn't it. She spoke of phone bills. I said they were a sore point with me, too. She used a most un-Maggie like expression.

'Do you know who you're talking to?' I asked.

'No,' she said uncertainly, halting in mid-flow.

'Thank heaven for that,' I told her and went back to my shaving.

The great thing about starting the week with an encounter like that, apart from its raw charm, of course, is that things can only get better. One thing has always puzzled me about wrong numbers, though. They're never engaged.

You may form the impression from all this that I'm anti-phone. Perish the thought. I'm nothing of the sort. Frustrated by the phone, yes. Bemused by it, yes. But some of my enduring mem-ories are phone-based and where would I be without them?

Now you may believe this, or you may not, but it's true. A man went into a crowded pub where there was only one barman serving, and, as is usual in these cases, his eye was as elusive as a Lough Neagh eel. There was a time, of course, when you could wave a pound note in the air and catch the curate's eye that way, but the pound coin lacks both the eye-catching and purchasing powers of the old-time note.

The clamouring throng of thirsty citizens barely heard the phone ring but they fell silent when the barman put it down, pulled three pints, placed them on a tray and raised the flap of the counter.

They parted before him like the Red Sea for the Israelites and every eye followed his progress to a table by the door. Every mind wondered what influence those three customers had. They had no influence at all, as it turned out, but one of them had a portable phone and knew the pub's number. So, he just phoned their order through to the counter. He knew, as we all know, that nobody ignores a ringing phone.

Actually I think that mobile phones are great crack, and a source of much enlightenment to a confirmed people-watcher like me. For example, I was standing looking at the day once and a small procession of cars passed. The driver of the first one had a look of amazement on his face, and the driver of the second one had his head out of the window, all the better to see the goings-on. The rest just tootled along in a resigned sort of way. They couldn't see what was happening and maybe it was just as well.

There was a man walking in the middle of the road at the head of the procession. A century ago, when horsepower was restricted mostly to horses, he would have been carrying a red flag. Since those days, walking down the middle of the road in this or any other country is indulged in only by those with a kamikaze streak or persons under the influence of recreational chemicals. Or, in this instance, a man with a mobile phone.

I don't often get the chance to do a bit of phone-watching on the hoof, but I have to tell you it's pretty much the same mixture as the static version. The telephone has a lot of limitations, and some of them become apparent when it comes to describing the size or shape of something. If you don't believe me, keep your eyes open the next time you see somebody making a call from a box, and see if you can interpret the tic-tac. Better still, watch yourself doing it.

Well, your man in the middle of the road was doing all the gestures and grinning all over his face. He looked a right idiot but he didn't know it because he was so busy signalling to the world that he was a very important idiot indeed.

The driver of the leading car eventually decided he'd had enough of this mobile entertainment and gave a blast on the horn. But did your man step smartly to one side? He did not. He drifted gradually towards the kerb, protected by his own pomposity from grievous bodily harm by irate road users.

There's something about mobile phones that seems to fill a

heartfelt inner want for some folk. You can hardly find a Sunday supplement these days that's not extolling the virtues of instant communication, anywhere, any time. For a modest outlay of many hundreds but ending reassuringly in 99p you can be contacted no matter where you are. This comes under the heading of A Very Good Thing. Especially for Very Important People.

I don't know any Very Important People. Anybody who knows me is by definition excluded from the Very Important category. The people I do business with come somewhere below that vital classification and they can never be contacted. They are protected from the importunities of lesser mortals by a phalanx of secretaries – well, actually, one secretary constitutes an impenetrable barrier in most cases – whose stock response is, 'Can you hold on a wee second till I see if he's in?'

Since the office is barely large enough to accommodate two people, the only seeing involved is whether he wants to speak to one of the lower orders or not. If he happens to have his head wedged into a comfortable corner while he dozes off the excesses of the night before, he's not in. A fellow like that isn't a potential customer for a mobile phone. He'd have to answer it himself. And, of course, Very Important People do all their business eyeball-to-eyeball with other Very Important People, so they don't need mobile phones either.

That leaves only posers as customers, and they might, just might, be dummies.

What I mourn the most in the telephone revolution is the demise of the old red phone boxes with their Button A and Button B phones. They were a useful source of small change for craftier members of the public in the olden days. One of my student contemporaries used to claim that he could get the price of ten cigarettes many a day just by pressing Button B in every phone box he passed and scooping the pennies left behind by impatient or absent-minded callers. Mischievous persons could also amuse themselves by leaving a drop of indian ink under Button B. I don't wish to discuss how I know that.

The end of the road for old red boxes also meant the end of those looks of resigned despair on the faces of the queue as the caller laid out a selection of small change, placed the cigarettes and matches beside that and proceeded to dial the number. I shall cherish forever the scene at an Antrim Road phone box when a woman went through the whole rigmarole of getting ready for a long call and then found she couldn't manage the phone and light her cigarette at the same time.

She pushed open the door and indicated to the sheepskin-coated, furbooted lady next in line that she wanted a light. The sheepskin-coated one, with market-trader stamped all over her, took a deep drag of her cigarette, then ground it into the pavement thoroughly and venomously.

'I do not smoke,' she told the caller grimly.

I wonder if Alexander Graham Bell, inventor of the crossed line and patron saint of the wrong number, ever stopped to think during his lifetime of just what he had inflicted on the human race? Of course, it's too late to ask him now. His number has been unobtainable since 1922.

4 *A Medical Education*

Everyone should spend some time in a doctor's waiting room. As a source of enlightenment it's hard to beat. I know that there are fastidious people about who might worry about picking up germs from the sick people but between ourselves I don't think there's much risk of that. The sick people, as they used to say in the old Petty Sessions courts, are going about their lawful occasions elsewhere. The majority of the clientele are there just out of habit, or in pursuit of a letter that will wring tears, or money, from the DHSS, or to lend moral support to somebody else on a similar mission. You may chance a visit without any risk whatever to your physical well-being.

My own medical education was greatly enhanced by a minor irritation that involved the doctor peering into my ear with a sophisticated instrument and being unable to see daylight. My affliction was not so serious that I couldn't hear the isolated snatches of conversation that have fuelled my imagination since.

'I didn't see you here last week, Maggie,' said one sufferer to another.

'Nah,' Maggie replied. 'I was bad last week and I couldn't get out.'

Bad, in this instance, meant sick. Of course, Maggie may have been involved in some form of rascality and was under house arrest as a result. I furtively assessed her, diagnosed illness, real or imaginary, and tucked the experience away in the recesses of my memory. There is something splendidly Irish and reassuringly idiotic in staying away from the doctor because of illness.

It reminded me of the way they used to do things in ancient China. I was never in ancient China, of course, nor nearer to modern China than a Chinese restaurant but I recall reading somewhere that in ancient China people paid the doctor only as long as they were well. They stopped paying up when they fell ill. I studied Maggie for evidence of oriental blood but there was none that I could see. Appearances can be deceptive, though, and I was mindful of a local broadcaster who achieved fame, if not fortune, by inventing an Irish family who emigrated to China. They opened a chain of Irish restaurants in that distanct, mysterious land and each was called The Poison Glen.

On my other hand, two men morosely discussed life's ups and

downs. Mostly downs, when I come to think of it, for a lot of their acquaintances seemed to be leaving this vale of tears.

'What's wrong with Joe?' one asked the other after a brief silence.

'Joe who?'

Sad to relate, Joe was no relation to Dr. Who, just a fellow who lived up in Whatchamacallit, which is apparently in the neighbourhood of the Springfield Road.

'There's nothing wrong with him. He always looked like that,' was the cryptic summary of Joe's appearance.

Both these patients had worked for the same firm at different times and shared a common loathing of the foreman. The way they told it, his parents had never bothered with the formality of matrimony.

'He was a rogue,' one of them remarked. If that seems mild, try inserting a popular local expletive in front of 'rogue,' the way the speaker did, and you'll get a sharper image.

'If he wasn't,' the other growled, 'he should have sued somebody about thon face of his.'

'So and so Boss's man,' the first one added, 'that's all he was.'

'He never mucked me about,' said the second one. 'He tried it but he ended up in the Ormeau Road.'

The waiting room population digested this revelation in silence. I took a close interest in a notice detailing what to do in the case of a fire but actually I was grappling with the picture of the smallish man hurling another whose face could form the basis of a lawsuit into the middle of a busy thoroughfare. From several streets away, too, judging by the tone.

The reality was disappointing. The foreman had ended up facing the boss in the Ormeau Road office, if, of course, that was what really happened. With the price of drink what it is these days, the doctor's waiting room may have replaced the pub as the place to air fantasies.

On my next visit my right hand neighbour in the queue was a robustly healthy-looking female critic of the National Health Service. The hospital just wouldn't take her serious illness seriously enough, so she was back to see what her own doctor was going to do about it.

'They wanted me to eat more fruit,' she complained to me. 'Did you ever?'

'I never did,' I said piously.

'And here's me, with a . . . a . . . what d'you call them hernias you get up here?' and she tapped herself menacingly on the chest. I was tempted and I gave in to temptation.

'Herbaceous,' I replied. May I be forgiven for this piece of medical sabotage but you have to pass the time somehow in the doctor's waiting room.

'Of course,' she went on, 'he was only a wee fella from up the country.'

I felt I had served a sufficiently long apprenticeship to be able to diagnose her illness. It was a bad case of the Here Be Dragons Syndrome. This lady distrusted everybody and everything originating beyond the end of the tramlines. Out in that mysterious uncharted world, marked by the ancient mapmakers as the domain of dragons, people learned their medicine from horse-doctors and witch-doctors. They couldn't be competent to diagnose the sophisticated illnesses of city folk. All this she imputed to the doctor with the accent who wanted her to eat more fruit instead of curing her with a piece of paper, the way a proper doctor would.

'Are you waiting to see the nurse?' she demanded.

'I am,' I admitted.

'Why?' she wanted to know.

'Because she's prettier than the doctor,' I told her, with as much naivete as I could muster.

'Next,' a voice called, and Mrs. Next abandoned the interrogation.

'Good luck with the herbaceous hernia,' I said to her as she went in. I hope she didn't tell the doctor who it was who introduced horticulture into her gullet. I'll need his services again.

While she was pouring out her assorted woes, the nurse, with the aid of a huge syringe, blew the cobwebs out of my ear. In a perverse sort of a way I missed that ear complaint. I could no longer turn it in the direction of requests to do things I felt disinclined to do. It also deprived my friends of the opportunity to alternately mouth silently and shout at me, before falling about laughing.

Two women with pushchairs made their leisurely way out ahead of me and, new-fangled with my restored, all-round hearing, I couldn't help eavesdropping.

'Late,' says he, I'll show ye late, wee girl,' said one. 'And he charged out of the house and away like the clappers.'

'And did he not get his tea?' asked the other half of the conversation.

'Oh, aye, he got chips in Glengormley.'

There's a whole disjointed world out there and I'm not part of it any more.

5 *Barney*

The dividing line between the world inhabited by writers and total insanity is a thin one, so when I saw a fellow rambling round with a python round his neck like a scarf I was only mildly surprised. Nobody else at the party seem in the least interested, being engaged in wolfing down sausage rolls and sinking endless glasses of paint-stripper loosely described as wine.

The python was called Cleo and the fellow who was wearing her was only a good friend, no more. There was a lady hovering in the background watching me watching the pair of them, and she introduced herself to me as the creature's owner, or mistress or whatever the appropriate expression is. She described Cleo as a wee pet and offered to demonstrate her affectionate qualities by detaching her from her current mode of transport and draping her round my neck.

I declined. Once in my colourful career I met a snake face to face, as it were, as it impersonated a length of heavy-duty electrical cable in the storage compartment of a compressor I was in charge of. Snakes are not slippery, like eels. I'm in a position to say this, though our acquaintance was brief, for by the time it had hit the ground I was many yards away and going strong.

Now this snake lady enlightened me about several aspects of snakedom. It seems the creatures can pine away, go off their food, and even develop complexes, go into a decline or develop the vapours, just like people. I realise that I'm doing less than justice to the technical expertise of a dedicated animal-lover, and they don't come more dedicated than those who love snakes. She had actually adopted stern measures to make Cleo toe the line. She had force-fed her.

'How,' I asked, in awe, 'do you force-feed a snake?'

'With great difficulty,' she informed me.

I suppose I asked for that. I've never gone in much for pets myself, so I lack the insight and enthusiasm of the truly committed. While I have never willingly gone out of my way to widen my acquaintance of the animal kingdom, there has been an assortment of animals over the years that have insinuated themselves into my company.

Well, there was Jaws, a member of the goldfish species. He, she or it – these fine distinctions are of interest only to another goldfish – was won by a junior member of the clan at a fair. No fisherman with arms outstretched and his mouth full of lies could have been more proud of a fishy acquisition.

It arrived, as these creatures do, in a plastic bag with handles, and it was clear from a very early stage that more elaborate accommodation would have to be provided. A jam jar or coffee jar was ruled out as being too cramped and like to draw down the wrath of the RSPCA on our hapless heads. Some mirthful speculation about Jaws getting on the phone to the cruelty people failed to divert attention from the fact that although he/she/it had cost nothing, money would soon have to change hands to keep the new arrival in the style to which the creature clearly expected to become accustomed.

A tank was duly installed on the top of a bookcase facing the television and his Nibs took to swimming around in a disdainfully detached manner. Then his young master decreed that the whole appearance of the thing was too spartan, so more money changed hands and a bridge was installed for Jaws to swim under and a wide selection of multi-coloured artificial underwater ferns for him to skulk among.

Pebbles of every shape, size and hue were added and his superior, detached residence began to look like the Lost City of Atlantis. I was rapidly achieving privileged customer status at the local pet shop.

Then the Loneliness Theory was evolved. Jaws would like company, I was told. I wasn't given the basis of this theory, just the bill for another goldfish – in advance. Junior's free prize was rapidly becoming a very expensive acquisition indeed. Jaws Two was duly installed late one evening. Early the next morning the newcomer was floating belly-up on the surface of the water, and no explanation was forthcoming from the original resident of the tank.

The Loneliness Theory collapsed. Jaws wasn't the sociable kind, but he was a right nuisance, because his tank had to be cleaned out and the water changed, either by Herself or myself, while his young master confined himself to a supervisory role. Or wasn't there at all.

Jaws continued to enjoy the best of grub and an excellent view of the television until the fateful day when somebody decided that a bit of mirror on the bottom of the tank would enhance his lifestyle considerably. First down the next morning discovered that he had popped his watery clogs during the night.

Perhaps he had seen himself in the mirror for the first time and the shock was too much for him. Maybe he thought his reflection was another interloper and he had cracked his skull in an effort to get at it like the previous one. Who knows? His passage went unlamented on any noticeable scale. There's a distinct lack of warmth in fish, unless properly cooked and served with chips.

The Cat came next. It arrived, mouthing silently, on the living-room window one Autumn afternoon and I indicated, with a lordly sweep of the hand, that it should take itself off forthwith. It remained unmoved. I went to the kitchen door to emphasise the instruction and there it was, all smarmy, rubbing against the door-frame. The split second I opened the door it vaulted nimbly forward.

I placed my foot against the door-frame to bar its way and instantly found that I had made a major mistake. Inside a split second a hissing, spitting, furry ball of fury was clinging to my shoe. The Cat was establishing the ground rules very early on.

It was, without exception, the worst-tempered animal I've ever come across. That furry brute would have eaten every single thing put in front of it and as a parting gesture savaged the provider. Interested parties claiming they would love a cat for their very own, came, saw, attempted to make friends and were scratched for their pains. All departed, muttering 'Thanks, but no thanks.'

We were torn between a desire to kill it and another to atone for the cruelty it had obviously suffered at other hands. It continued to hoover up the best brands of cat food at an astonishing rate and scratch every member of the family who attempted to pat its belligerent head. It lived in a box in the yard and devoted all its non-eating, non-scratching, non-sleeping hours to working its way into the house. We successfully denied it access.

It finally left of its own accord, vanquished by a kitten the size of a well-worn tennis ball splattered with black ink. It followed Herself from the bus-stop one day, so close behind her that she couldn't spot where the noise was coming from.

And the noise was considerable. That creature had a noise several sizes too big for it and a tenacity of spirit that called for recognition and reward. It stood on its hind legs on the front step and decreed that it would be heard. With one warlike feline already on the grocery-list we weren't in the market for another, however winsome, but this one neatly solved all our dilemmas by scurrying up the drive of the house next door, through the hedge and taking up residence in The Cat's box.

That was before it spotted that The Cat hadn't finished its breakfast. It shot out of the box, polished off every pick of food, stood on the plate and licked off most of the pattern before working its way over the edge and tackling the design underneath. The Cat returned at this point, ready for battle and I wondered how it would be possible to save the kitten from the wrath that was about to come.

There was no wrath, no risk to life or limb. After a ritual bout of hissing and threatening, The Cat simply stalked off and never returned.

Which left us with Bunty, who grew up to be marginally more civilised, and with a blue folder full of her veterinary history and accompanying dents in Herself's bank account. Not, you will note, in mine.

She became part of the household though she didn't exactly endear us to the neighbours due to the local tomcats' refusal to recognise that she been spayed, as a neighbouring child put it, to prevent her having pups.

She and I lived in a state of armed neutrality for the best part of a couple of years, then history repeated itself. One day another feline tennis-ball, ink-spattered, turned up out of nowhere and refused to go away. I suppose the garden was big enough for both of them but Bunty didn't see it that way and neither did Herself.

As things turned out, no action was necessary. Bunty huffed, puffed, hissed, spat and took to staying out all night, coming back later and later in the morning until one day she didn't show up at all. Two days afterwards the children from up the street came back from their holidays and reclaimed their runaway kitten. There was remarkably little grief on any side.

This wasn't true in the rabbit's case. He was nominally the property of our youngest son but his day to day care was the responsibility of Herself and myself. Like Jaws, he came free, as a present, and like Jaws, his accommodation was a costly affair. He needed a hutch and that had to be constructed in such a way that Barney – which was the somewhat rakish name we bestowed on him – could come and go without being followed by the local dogs and cats intent on having him for breakfast.

He was an object of interest to every dog for miles around. They blundered into the gardens on either side and stood with their paws on the walls and their tongues hanging out. The neighbours gritted their teeth and pretended it was all right, really.

It fell to me to erect a wire mesh enclosure around his residence, enclosing a sufficient area for him to roam about and thumb his nose at the dogs. When you take into account the materials for the hutch, the wire mesh and the fence posts, Barney rapidly became an expensive hobby. The owner of the local builders' suppliers put his tongue in his cheek and talked of changing his car a month or two earlier than he had planned.

No sooner was the fence completed than he began to tunnel below it and cavort in March hare madness through the neighbouring gardens with the dogs in hot and destructive pursuit.

I took the fence down and re-erected it with about six inches of the mesh sunk in the ground. He resumed his burrowing at a deeper level. I dropped the fence another bit. He took to leaping off the roof of the hutch and over the fence.

More wire to close off the top of the enclosure clinched it for the man at the builders' suppliers. He changed the car.

Barney continued to escape and I continued to recapture him. It became increasingly difficult, because he wasn't a tame creature really, just the offspring of a tame female and a trespassing wild male.

I must dispel a myth about rabbits at this stage. They're not as cuddly and fluffy as you might think. Barney never actually bit me, though he bared his teeth at me a time or two, but he did scratch me with sufficient vigour to draw blood more than once. He wasn't exactly flavour of the month with me after the first scratch . . . and no pun is intended.

At first he confined his marauding to our own side of the street but one day he discovered Utopia and a vegetable garden on the other side became home from home for him. It took the combined efforts of the owner, his wife and myself, along with a length of redundant net curtain which we threw over him, to get him back into solitary confinement.

He had to go. That was what he wanted anyway, so I put him in the car and we all set off in the general direction of Glenavy. It was all very solemn, just like a funeral, and nobody was more solemn than the one who had been deprived of the dubious joys of rounding him up, day in and day out. I kept my views to myself. I didn't want to say anything that might be held against me at some future date.

I rather liked the idea of getting back the full use of my back garden. I looked forward to not having to career through my neighbours' gardens in competition with a posse of dogs, just to head off a kamikaze rabbit. A rabbit-free future had attractions for me, all right.

Well, we turned him loose at a suitable point and he took off like something out of a cartoon film. Before we were all in the car he had come hopping back and sat looking at us from the other side of the field-gate. I looked at the others. They looked at me. For the first time in his furry, chaotic life he came home willingly.

Three days later a passing car put a stop to his career as he went on his thieving way to the vegetable garden. Which was a pity really. Cleo would love to have met him, I'm sure.

6 *Snap-happy*

The first camera I ever possessed was a miniature job that you could have almost but not quite hidden in your closed fist. It cost ten shillings, which not only dates me and it, but brings us all back a decade or two.

I was at school at the time, a boarding establishment, and cameras were frowned on. This prohibition was hard to understand, unless the authorities feared an epidemic of smuggled films exposing conditions in the place.

My camera was the product of a Japanese company which had, I believe, been in the brush-making trade until the Americans decided World War Two had gone on long enough and put the company out of business.

The versatile Orientals, for their own inscrutable reasons, turned their brush-making ingenuity to cameras. Their first efforts were less than impressive, because it took some time before the term Japanese became synonymous with quality. My camera came somewhere in the second wave of effort. It was durable. Tiny it may have been but it weighed more than the average pocket could stand for long.

Films were not available locally. You got half a dozen with the camera. They were extra, naturally, but a camera without film isn't much of an investment; something that both the Japanese and the mail order company knew instinctively. I ordered the obligatory half a dozen. They were not money well spent.

The camera looked a scaled-down modern SLR job. It only looked like one. It didn't perform like one. The wind-on knob, for example, was the most stubborn mechanism ever made. The only solution, in the early stages, was to take the snap, then wedge the knob in a door and turn the camera.

Given the footery size of the camera, bleeding knuckles accompanied each photograph. When the need for a door to wind on the film was taken into account, furtive photography was out of the question. The first spool of film was a completely forgettable experience.

I fared rather better with the second. I took it at home and used pliers to encourage the wind-on mechanism. The snag was that although the knob was turning, the film wasn't always doing the same. The result was a rash of double exposures. When the second batch came back from the chemist and featured a touchy female relative with a thorn bush growing out of her lap, I called it a day and wrote the whole kit off to experience.

I have owned a variety of cameras since then and they have all, at one time or another, dropped me in it at critical moments. This is partly due to the fact that since that time I have tended to rely on automatic cameras that thought for themselves and therefore for me. I never enquired too closely into their countries of origin but I suspect that none of them was Japanese. Except the last one. I suspect a sinister connection between it and the first one, the one that needed a door frame to function properly.

This last one had a famous name and wonderfully efficient electronics. It was idiot-proof. In fact it was proof against all mortal failings, except being dropped on a shop floor in Donegal. The only thing functioning after that was the red light that indicated a healthy battery. It blinked like a thing possessed, though I wasn't asking it to. It finally blinked out and the whole complex machine became a lump of junk.

'Beyond repair,' was the considered verdict of the repair shop though they offered to send it away for an expensive and potentially useless second opinion. The only function left was its capacity to burn up batteries while you waited. Even that fizzled out in the end.

There's a widespread belief that toothache disappears the minute you step into the dentist's waiting room. The Japanese, wily and ingenious, have built this capacity into their cameras.

When I responded to the insurance company's request to bring it in for inspection, I brought along a set of batteries. I fully expected it to burn them out under the inspector's eyes. He popped them in and the thing began to function like new, in a splendid example of Murphy's Law.

It was a Shinto curse on me, I know, for hurling my first Japanese camera and four films into the bin along with a string of Western swear words.

I'm glad in a way that my first camera and its supply of film didn't survive. It ensured that I didn't join the ranks of the Great School Photograph Bores. I'm not referring here to the modern, neat, four-small-plus-one-large package deals which feature only your own offspring in living, riotous colour. The true School Photograph is an abomination a yard long – or perhaps it only seems so – six inches deep because millimetres hadn't been invented when it was taken, and encased in a mournful, black frame.

It's in black and white and features perhaps two hundred and fifty bodies, each surmounted by a face about the size of a slightly swollen full stop. Some of these people will have achieved fame in past decades as concert violinists, professors of anthropology or urban guerrillas.

Others will, of course, have shuffled off their mortal coils, but most will, like the owner of this historic record, have attained total obscurity. Unlike him, however, they are imprisoned in the frame and he is not. He, indeed, is dangling The School Photograph in front of your stricken eyes and preparing to give you the third degree.

'Do you know anybody in that photograph?' he asks you.

This is a trick question of the lowest possible sort. He is somewhere in that ancient blur of humanity, but by no stretch of the imagination could you connect any of these minute and skinny persons with the Michelin Man lookalike into whose hands you and the photograph have fallen. You can say you're hopeless at this sort of thing. You can say it but it won't do you any good. 'Ah, come on,' he'll say, 'sure I haven't changed that much.'

Not much. The photograph was taken in the spring of 1947 and everyone in it has a full head of hair and full mouthful of teeth, a tribute to the spartan diet of those halcyon days.

It's a curious thing but nobody you went to school with yourself ever produces a copy of The School Photograph. That way you would have a starting point. You could locate yourself, because you haven't changed all that much though everyone else has. You're lost with this one. Is he among the seniors grinning ferociously from their perches in the back row or among the first years squatting tailor-fashion with elbows resting on scarred knees in the front?

If you opt for the back row and he's in the front you've also opted for making him five years older than he really is and that's no way to make friends and influence people. If you place him, with a wild guess, in the front row, he'll never forgive you for failing to identify the vision and maturity that place him firmly among the elder statesmen in the back row.

The odds are about two hundred and fifty to one against getting him right but there is a bright side to all this. You'll never be asked back and who needs that kind of hassle anyway? And at the first hint of another host producing his School Photograph, complete fabrications about broken or lost reading glasses will spring unbidden to your lips.

Nothing, however, can insulate you against the truly awesome experience of the Wedding Photographs. From every art and part, from their mountain fastnesses and haunts across the seas, the female relatives arrive in droves, to see and be seen, and to upstage relatives not seen since the last family gathering. And like the camp-followers of a conquering army the male relatives, cleaned, polished, shining and reluctant, bring up the rear with the ragged enthusiasm of men who want nothing more than a quiet corner of the bar but know in their hearts that it will be denied them.

You won't know a single face among this multitude frozen in time. It is even possible to get the chief participants in these dramas mixed up and I speak as one who knows. I hold the record for clanger-dropping while punch-drunk from an endless panorama of wedding photographs.

Herself was present on this occasion and I caught a wait-till-I-get-you-home look in her eye that put it in my mind to display a totally false enthusiasm. I picked up a photograph depicting a stunned looking, apparently elderly person in the neighbourhood of the bride.

'And this,' I said brightly, 'will be the bride's father?'

It was the groom, who was brother to the photographer, who was displaying his handiwork for our entertainment. As they used to say in the Victorian novels, let us draw a veil over the subsequent proceedings.

7 *An Inspector Falls*

Miss Henry radiated the authority of an imperial gunboat showing the flag to turbulent natives. Presumably she had a first name but no one, friend or foe, would have dared to use it. She was the principal of a two-teacher school in sparsely populated farm country and she ran it by a set of rules, unwritten and unquestioned, that owed nothing to any official guidelines.

No attendance officer, for example, had ventured near her establishment since the never-to-be-forgotten day when one such official, emerging already shaken, found the lane leading to the main road carpeted with broken bottles. He was not in the least cheered by a row of grinning faces at the windows.

Much thunderous knocking ensued before Miss Henry opened the door and enquired, in far from friendly tones, what he wanted this time. He told her that some evilly-disposed person had littered his escape route with broken glass when he was in the school on his lawful business. She viewed him with the expression of one who has stepped in something nasty and expressed the ominous hope that he didn't think she had anything to do with it. He grovelled. She said, 'well, then,' and prepared to close the door.

He asked for the loan of a brush to clear a puncture-free path to the road. Miss Henry informed him that the brushes were in the domain of the part-time cleaner, with whom she had a long-standing agreement. The cleaner didn't teach and she, for her part, didn't do any cleaning. She permitted the luckless official a final, tantalising glimpse of the cleaning equipment in an alcove facing the door. Then she shut him out of her sight and left him to clear a path for his car by whatever means he chose.

When she drove sedately out in her ancient Ford that afternoon, the broken glass had disappeared as mysteriously as it had come. A rural parent settling an old score with officialdom caused her no surprise. She had never made the slightest attempt to conceal her own dislike of petty bureaucrats from her pupils, or anyone else for that matter, and her own attitude to attendance and time-keeping was well known to be flexible.

Some of her pupils had their quota of farm chores to do before school and at times would have to stay at home all day to help. She didn't see this as any kind of pretext for official breast-beating.

Instead, she operated a kind of balancing act, sometimes working on past the official closing time, at others finishing early.

This approach won general acceptance in the community. A few parents disapproved but held their peace. There were no known cases of anyone winning an argument with Miss Henry. In fact, no one could remember an instance of anyone having started one with her either.

Not, that is, until Richard Arthur Thompson arrived on the scene. He firmly believed that everyone was up to something and it was his dearest wish to catch them at it. This wasn't what the education authority paid him to do. They just wanted him to visit schools and establish on behalf of the taxpayers that the education of the young was proceeding in a satisfactory manner. They would have preferred that relations between their inspector and the schools in this area were cordial. This was the attitude at the highest level. It was pretty much the same at the lowest level, where the teachers struggled with varying degrees of success against the encroaching tides of ignorance.

At the middle level, where Richard Arthur Thompson functioned, things were not so simple. Order was his god and he was its prophet. His orthodox soul yearned for the totalitarian efficiency of an educational system in which he could look at his watch at ten o'clock of a morning and know that, in schools up and down the land, paragraph two of a composition on spring was just beginning. He longed to eradicate the tedious complications that children and ruggedly individualistic teachers brought into education.

It was one of his less endearing practices, when visiting a country school, to drive smartly past, park in a convenient field gate and then double back on foot in the hope of finding out that no education was taking place. He would bend low passing the windows and, ignoring the protocol that required him to call first with the head teacher, he would burst into the classroom of his choice. The startled reaction his mode of arrival always caused was a source of great satisfaction to him.

It was this Indian scout approach that led indirectly to his confrontation with Miss Henry. He was creeping past the staff-room window of a school some miles from hers one morning when the headmaster, who was in there having a quiet smoke, chose that moment to drop his cigarette end out of the window. It fell on his hat and travelled, smouldering, as he continued his crabwise progress down the side of the building, pausing with ear cocked at each window for sounds of revelry and mayhem.

From his vantage point at the staffroom window the headmaster watched him until he reached the end of the building and turned towards the side entrance. It was the inspector's turn to be startled as he came tip-toeing along the corridor and met the headmaster, smug and self-righteous, with hand outstretched in welcome.

As they entered the headmaster's room, Richard Arthur removed his hat and the cigarette end fell to the floor, where it was crushed and kicked out of sight with an adroit flick of the teacher's shoe.

The headmaster thought it prudent to warn Miss Henry of the inspector's presence in the district, for he knew that Richard Arthur, deprived of blood in one school, was sure to seek it elsewhere and she was the nearest potential victim. He hastily scribbled the word 'Inspector' on a piece of paper and dispatched a cycle-owning pupil with it to Miss Henry's school. Richard Arthur, who had more eyes than most people, had observed this furtive transaction and was glad, because he could see the school gate from where he stood and he knew something the headmaster didn't. The messenger had departed on foot. He had chosen that day not to bring his bike to school but the boy was no fool. If he had revealed this information someone else would have got the lengthy break from lessons.

Richard Arthur Thompson, the all-wise and all-seeing, continued with his inspection, content in the knowledge that while the headmaster might think his note had been delivered and the messenger was on his way back, he knew differently. After a reasonable interval he took his leave and caught up with the messenger who was still a long way from his destination.

'I'll deliver that note for you,' he told the lad. 'You can trot along back to school.'

He marched triumphantly into Miss Henry's class for the first time and handed her the note. She trawled up her spectacles from where they reposed on her ample frontage at the end of a chain. She read the single word, peered over her glasses at Richard Arthur, then back at the note. She let the spectacles ski downhill to the end of their chain before addressing him.

'I know you're an inspector,' she said, making the word sound leprous, 'Why did you feel you had to write it down?'

Richard Arthur sensed at once that he was in the presence of a dedicated and methodical hater. Once on the wrong side of her, he realised, and you would have to stay there. The battle lines would have to be drawn over a worthwhile issue.

It looked as if the Basins Affair might prove to be the very thing. Among the delusions he cherished was the conviction that there was large-scale misappropriation of school stationery and equipment. In his bizarre world, teachers' houses were full of purloined exercise books and pencils, so he conducted spot-checks on the annual requisition for schools in his area. Miss Henry had ordered, among numerous other items, three enamel basins for cookery lessons. They came in a single carton from the suppliers, separate from the rest of the order.

Two or three days after they came, Richard Arthur Thompson, public watchdog, duly turned up to check them. The carton was solemnly placed on Miss Henry's desk, he sat on her chair, opened his brief case and produced a bulging file from which he extracted the carbon copy of her order for three enamel basins. He studied the document at length, he fished about in the carton for the advice note, he compared the two sheets of paper in menacing silence. Then he took the basins out of their cartons.

The children were fascinated by this grown man who had driven twenty-five miles to count three basins. Miss Henry, breathing heavily at one side of her usurped desk, added to the dramatic effect. Richard Arthur Thompson finally spoke.

'Miss Henry,' he said. 'there are only two basins here.'

He was a happy man at that moment. He had finally caught somebody at something. When the somebody was the formidable Miss Henry, flouter of rules and scourge of officialdom, his cup indeed ran over. In his mind's eye he saw the government's basin in her kitchen. All the joyous arrears of discipline were about to be called in. He savoured the moment.

She leaned over and picked up the basins. It was true. There were only two. The order said three. The advice note said three. She knew there were three. But the evidence said two.

'Now,' said Richard Arthur Thompson, ace detective, 'where do you suppose the third one is?'

A tight little smile flirted with his lips as she picked up, first one and then the other, peering into each and into the carton in bafflement. He tapped the advice note with his pen. He shook his head sadly. He looked the very model of trust betrayed. Already he was composing comments about a fine career ignominiously ended . . . and for what? A basin?

Just then a small girl ambled up and lifted one of the basins. She thrust her forefinger nail against the rim and revealed that it was really two enamel basins, hot off the maker's line and so tightly jammed one inside the other as to look like one.

'These two are stuck together, sir,' said the little girl, somewhat unnecessarily. Miss Henry said nothing, in her unmistakable way. Richard Arthur Thompson, foiled again, said nothing either. He merely gathered up his papers and departed, amid the monstrous and unholy joy of Miss Henry's pupils.

A less tenacious man would have admitted defeat but fortune smiled and sent him an anonymous note, the work of a disgruntled parent. It alleged that Miss Henry was in the habit of coming late to school, and of leaving early. It remarked that the trifling amount of work she did between arrival and departure in no way justified the enormous salary she was paid. The letter ended with a blunt request. What were those in high places going to do about this scandalous state of affairs?

The author struck the right note for Richard Arthur Thompson, because he was fond of invading schools five or ten minutes after classes had started, in the hope of catching latecoming teachers. He sometimes varied this practice by turning up five minutes before school ended, just in case any of the staff should be sneaking out early. As a newcomer to the area he was unfamiliar with Miss Henry's time-table juggling activities. As far as he was concerned, the letter-writer had the facts right.

He arrived one morning at five to nine and found her at her desk marking exercise books. He mouthed some platitudes about the weather. She was still smarting from the Basins Affair and ignored him. He hung around uncertainly until the class came in, then he took a perfunctory look at the exercise books and departed. He came back a few days later at five minutes to three and found the place in the throes of an art lesson that went on until after four. This time everybody ignored him.

He decided on the false security ploy and stayed away for a whole month. On his next swoop he arrived at half-past eight and found Miss Henry dealing with a mound of paperwork. He squeezed himself into a child's desk at the back of the room, opened his briefcase and got on with his own.

Stony silence filled the room. He was rather relieved when the class came in and a small, grinning boy tugged his sleeve and indicated that he wanted his desk.

On the perfectly reasonable grounds that Miss Henry wouldn't expect lightning to strike twice he did exactly the same thing next morning. She seemed to have been on the premises all night. This time she let him settle uncomfortably into the desk by the door, then she rose from her own desk and bore down on him, an awesome spectacle indeed. She settled her considerable bulk on the desk in front.

'I think you should know,' she informed him 'that there is a great deal of speculation around here about just what the two of us get up to in an empty school every morning.'

Richard Arthur Thompson was pushing fifty and a thoroughly confirmed bachelor and Miss Henry was well satisfied with the effect her lie had on him. He opened his mouth and closed it several times. He turned a number of interesting shades of green and red. His teeth and tongue became hopelessly entangled. In ten seconds he seemed to reach pension age, and in another ten he was haring across the playground towards his car and liberty. Her derisory laughter vibrated the window panes of the empty building behind him.

He was never the same man after that. Some time passed before he was seen in the area again, and when he finally did re-appear his right ankle was encased in plaster. There was no reason to suppose that he was injured in anything other than an accident. However, the rumour soon spread that he had been heartbroken by his failure to seduce Miss Henry and tried to end it all by jumping off a cliff somewhere along the North Antrim coast. Some people were quite specific about the location. The rumours all agreed about one thing. The tide had been out at the time and he had only broken his ankle.

This was only said so that people could add that he couldn't even get that much right.

That, of course, was mere malice.

8 *Diversions in the Personal Columns*

Little amuses the innocent, my grandmother used to say, and far less the fool. I don't know which category she'd have put me in if she'd lived long enough to find out that I get much of my diversion in the personal columns of the press.

In a sense the exercise is academic but there's no reason why someone on a diet couldn't read a menu, is there? If I hadn't been motivated by a similar conviction I'd never have found out about the widowed lady who is, by her own admission, quite respectable, and looking for a respectable male person, view friendship, as the jargon of these things puts it.

Until I read that ad I had never even thought of looking up 'quite' in the dictionary. I thought I knew what it meant but I took down the big thick book with the hard covers for a quick brush-up on the definition. It was reassuring to find that 'quite' still meant 'fairly' or 'somewhat.' So here was a case of a somewhat respectable lady in search of a respectable man.

There's no pussyfooting around as far as his specifications are concerned. Fairly respectable won't do. Somewhat respectable is out. He must be respectable, full stop. He has to be well-to-do, decent, well-behaved, presentable and with good standing in the community.

Persons prone to slouch up to the corner shop of a morning, in slippers and string vest – and trousers, let us hope – to get the paper and a couple of baps need not reply to this ad. Neither should nattily-suited gents with furled umbrellas, an incremental post in the Civil Service and a few bob in the building society.

The first category won't pass muster. Prospective applicants from the second group should bear in mind that the second half of the deal is only 'quite' respectable and clearly reserves the right to stand at the front door in slippers and curlers ready to take on all comers. This might only be a faint possibility and 'quite' may cover a multitude of other excesses. However, the reservations expressed by that little word should have been enough to alert a hopeful lonely-heart to the risk of a lousy bargain.

Women, whether respectable or merely quite respectable, should think long and hard before offering to meet a character who describes himself as 'quite' friendly. Such persons claim to be thirty-five and are in the market for an unattached lady between thirty-eight and forty. The one I studied alleged that the view was friendship/marriage.

He wanted friendship, initially at any rate, but he was only prepared to be fairly, or somewhat, friendly in return. Such men are dangerous and in my view likely to set about their future in-laws, if things should progress to that point, with a cudgel or other blunt instrument. And why – the question has to be asked – did he want someone with a head start of three to five years anyway? Steer clear, that's my advice.

Another fellow's motives and tastes were even more questionable. He advertised for a 'genuine female.' He didn't, you will note, specify a female what. Having consorted with plumbers and other skilled persons in the course of my varied lifetime, I'm in a position to state that some items of plumbing hardware are variously known as 'male' and 'female.' Somehow, I don't think that an assortment of plumbing connections under plain brown wrapper and delivered to his box number was what he was after at all.

Neither do I imagine that he was in the market for unwanted snakes and other household pets of the wrong gender. Nor do I think that a dummy purloined from a boutique, cash on delivery or otherwise, would meet his requirements. Judging by the 'genuine' tag, somebody must already have tried that one. I think we may safely assume that your man wanted a woman. It is to be hoped that interested parties gave some thought to the way he described them before applying for the vacancy.

Then I came across an ad from a fellow who described himself as attractive and a car owner. As far as I know, if you take the halt, the lame, the blind, the too-young and the too-old and the couldn't care less out of the potential driving population of this country, there's a vehicle on the road for every two people. All right, some of them are juggernauts, some are bulldozers and an awful lot of the rest should be tipped into a disused quarry at dead of night, but vehicles all the same.

In the ordinary way I would counsel people to beware of persons describing themselves as attractive but this advertiser's self-effacing description possibly owed much to his assertion that he had the use of a holiday apartment in a continental resort for a week every year. Which may have something to do with the fact that he was advertising for an attractive girl for, wait for it . . . possible lasting friendship.

Do you suppose it was possible he just wanted the goods on a week's trial? Of course, I'm a mere innocent abroad in these matters. I may have done the man an injustice by harbouring such unworthy suspicions.

More interesting still was the widow in the market for a tall man. She wasn't specific about his long term prospects, indeed she didn't appear to care a jot or even tittle whether he was respectable, somewhat respectable, friendly or only moderately so, genuine or plastic, just so long as he was tall.

She sounded like someone who kept a lot of things on high shelves and, having done her sums, worked it out that an ad in the personal columns was a lot cheaper than buying a step-ladder. This is possibly how step-fathers got their name. You can gather enlightenment from many a source. All you need is an open mind.

Another ad that intrigued me, partly because it was right below the widow's appeal for a tall man, was inserted by a tall, extrovert, single male (human, not plumbing, in this case because he was a non-smoker) who was on the lookout for romance. People who describe themselves as extroverts should be approached with caution. It usually means they embarrass everybody around them in public. Leaving that caveat aside, how many points should he have rated for being a non-smoker? There was a time when it was the macho thing to do. Now it's the opposite.

I once saw a reference written by a man for a job applicant he didn't like but didn't want to refuse, either. It read simply, 'I have known this applicant for twenty years. He does not smoke.' I have always considered that to be a masterpiece of understatement. It is always to the forefront of my mind as I browse through the personal columns.

Apart from the implications of the non-smoking assertion, that advertiser seemed to have the right qualification for the widow. He was tall. He also had his own business, which could have been a useful plus if he had given more details. A modest size engineering works is one thing, but shamrock-grower, which might confer self-employed, business-owner status, is something else entirely.

Our non-smoking businessman, being an extrovert, would hardly have been impressed by these attempts to tie up loose ends. You see, he wanted a young girl. He offered no hint about his own age but we'll let that pass. And she had to be very attractive. Very attractive girls don't need the personal columns. And the widow, I almost forgot to add, claimed to be 'quite' presentable.

The last ad in that column really did give me a shock. 'Widows made to your own specifications. State size,' on closer inspection had wandered in from a different classification. And it was a misprint. 'Windows' was what was meant.

9 *A Friend in Need is a Pest*

They called him Sam about the village but it wasn't short for Samuel, which would have been logical. It was short for Samaritan, which wasn't a bit logical, but they were as economical with nicknames as with everything else, so when Sam was mentioned, everybody knew who was meant.

Nobody knew when or how he had acquired his biblical tag but everybody knew that he was the most neighbourly and obliging man in the district. If you needed the loan of a spade, or an extra hand with the sheep or the turf, or your car was out of action, you could always rely on Sam. In moments of disaster, real or imaginary Sam was the man people turned to.

He wasn't any kind of Holy Joe. The village had several of those, all well established. He was a small, nut-brown man with a whimsical sense of humour and a healthy measure of cynicism in his character. He didn't mind if news of his good deeds circulated freely, especially if there was a touch of the absurd about them. He enjoyed telling a story against himself, with his weatherbeaten face crinkled in glee and his brown eyes dancing below the peak of his cap.

The episode about Sam and the part he played in Daly's toothache have long since passed into legend. To hear him tell the story himself you would never think it was he and not Daly who got the treatment.

It began late on a Saturday night, or just into Sunday morning. He was standing, as he put it colourfully, in a puddle of his own trousers and rummaging for his pyjama jacket when the shock of the doorbell catapulted him into a tangled heap on the floor. By the time he had struggled upright the chimes had brought the dog into action, straining murderously at the end of its chain in the yard.

He found Jim Daly on the doorstep and his face was as long as a wet fortnight.

'I've got a terrible toothache,' he told Sam mournfully.

Sam was most things to most men and many an odd request brought people to his farmhouse a mile outside the village but there were some gaps in his vocational education. He mentioned one now.

'I'm not a dentist,' he told Daly.

'Aren't you the right comedian,' Daly growled. 'All I want you to do is drive me down as far as the doctor's.'

Daly was one of Nature's pedestrians. The courageous nephew who tried to teach him to drive had not only abandoned the attempt but threatened to join a monastery as well.

Sam pointed out a small difficulty in dealing with Daly's request.

'It's after midnight.' he said. 'The good doctor will be in bed after a hard Saturday afternoon's golf. I wouldn't want to be in the shoes of the man that would call on him at this hour of the night.'

The village had two doctors, but neither a dentist nor a chemist, and Dr. Higgins, who was Daly's doctor, was an irascible man who had a short way with people turning up with trivial complaints outside of surgery hours.

'And another thing,' Sam added, 'that's dentist's business.'

Daly recoiled in fright at the mention of the dentist.

"I'm going to no dentist, and that's that,' he snapped. 'All I want is a couple of painkillers. That'll do me fine. I don't suppose you . . .'

'There's not such a thing about the house,' Sam told him, for he never had ache or pain, 'but if you're hell-bent on suicide I'll drive you down to Dr. Higgins. And then, Jim, you're on your own.'

'That'll do for me,' said Daly gratefully and he fidgeted from foot to foot while Sam pulled on a sweater and trousers and brought the van round from the hayshed at the back. The journey to the doctor's house was punctuated by his facetious predictions about the reception Daly was likely to get.

The sufferer used almost as much vigour on the doctor's doorbell as he had on Sam's and when an upstairs window was finally flung open the voice that addressed them was far from civil.

'Who's that down there? Step back into the light so that I can see you. What do you want?' the doctor called down.

'It's me, Jim Daly, doctor,' Daly called up. 'I've got a terrible toothache.'

For the second time inside half an hour somebody informed Daly that he wasn't a dentist.

'Oh, I don't want it pulled, or anything,' Daly hastily assured the doctor, 'All I want is a couple of painkillers. That'll do the job.'

'Your teeth are a dentist's business,' Dr. Higgins crisply informed him. 'Dentists don't practise medicine and I don't interfere in their work. Go and see Joe Grimley in the morning.'

Joe Grimley, the nearest dentist, practised eight miles away.

'Tomorrow is Sunday,' Daly pointed out desperately.

Dr Higgins paused in the act of closing the window.

'There are two flaws in your argument,' he called down. 'First of all, today is Sunday. One o'clock on Sunday morning, to be exact. The second is that you seem to think it's all right to drag me out of bed, but not the dentist, when it's his business and not mine you're pestering me about.'

He slammed the window shut and left Daly standing mournfully on the step. Sam threw open the passenger door of the van.

'Get in,' he said. 'I know a great cure for toothache.'

He parked the van discreetly in the yard behind Scullion's pub and the pair of them cautiously approached the back door. This time Sam did the bell-ringing. Within seconds Scullion's tousled head appeared at an upstairs back window.

'What the hell are you two doing here?' he demanded in a loud whisper. 'It's one o'clock on Sunday morning.'

'We know the time,' Sam answered agreeably, 'and we know the day. But Daly here has a terrible toothache.'

'I'm not a dentist,' Scullion pointed out, reasonably and truthfully. Daly uttered a number of coarse expressions.

'If any other eejit tells me he's not a dentist this blessed and holy night,' he yelled, 'I'll kill him, I swear it, I'll kill him.'

'I thought,' Sam remarked to Scullion, 'that a shot of hot whiskey would do the trick. I've heard tell it's a powerful prescription for the toothache.'

'All right,' Scullion conceded, 'I'll be down in a tick.'

He admitted them to the back room, boiled the kettle and prepared the prescription. Sam and Scullion, teetotallers both, had a mug of tea apiece with the leftover water from the medicinal brew. Daly drank his hot whiskey with discreet enthusiasm.

'Well, how does it feel now?' Sam asked him.

'Sore as ever,' grumbled Daly.

'Give him another one,' Sam said to Scullion, and while Daly took his medicine manfully, the two benefactors discussed football. Daly finally set down his glass.

'Well?' they demanded in unison.

'Sore as hell,' slurred Daly through a foolish grin.

'Give him another one, Scullion,' said Sam. 'And you're paying for this one yourself, Daly.'

Daly paid for two more. Sam refused a second mug of tea. Scullion stood Daly a final hot whiskey on the house and by this time he was anaesthetised against everything except the toothache. It stubbornly resisted the treatment.

'Well,' said Sam, 'there's no point in any more of this and we've kept Scullion out of his bed long enough. We'll try another approach to this matter. We'll go to my doctor. He won't see us stuck.'

'Now, wait a minute,' Scullion interrupted. 'Daly's not his patient, you are. And you know that Dr. Clarke can't abide drink in any shape or form. And anyway, it's after two. If you bring this drunken hobo to his door at this hour there'll be ructions.'

'True enough,' Sam agreed. 'But what choice have we got?'

'Phone him from here,' Scullion suggested. 'Tell him it's you that has the toothache. Ask him to put a couple of pills in a wee box and leave them out on the step for you and you'll be down in a minute for them. That way he'll be none the wiser.'

'Now that's good thinking,' Sam said. 'We'll do it your way.'

Dr. Clarke answered his phone on the second ring. He was a voracious reader and was still up finishing a book. He was all concern for Sam even before he heard his problem. He rarely saw Sam in his professional capacity and he immediately assumed something serious was wrong.

'Ah, it's nothing,' Sam said. 'Just a raging toothache. I can't get a wink of sleep with it at all. It came on suddenly, otherwise I wouldn't dream of bothering you at this hour of the night. A couple of painkillers would do the job. If you would just put a couple in a box and leave them on the front step . . .'

'It's no trouble at all,' said Dr Clarke cheerfully, 'just come on down right away.'

Sam installed the stocious Daly in the passenger seat with Scullion's help and the publican peered furtively up and down the street for signs of police before he waved them out. They were the only living souls between the pub and Dr Clarke's.

Sam had been peering around the step for several seconds, looking for a tablet box, before he remembered that he hadn't had a chance to finish his request about leaving them outside. As he straightened up to consider his next move the door opened and Dr Clarke took his arm.

'Come on in,' he said, 'that's it, just in there to your right, step into the surgery, drop your trousers, you won't feel a thing.'

'But,' Sam stammered, 'tablets is all I want, a couple of painkillers, they'll do the job.'

'Nonsense, man,' said Dr Clarke, 'painkillers are no good in a case like this and anyway you won't be able to see Joe Grimley for the best part of thirty-six hours.'

'Ah, now, wait a minute,' Sam protested.

'Drop them,' commanded Dr Clarke, who stood well over six foot and exuded the kind of personal authority normally only found in sergeant-majors. For the second time that night Sam found himself standing in a puddle formed by his own trousers.

No syringe could possible be as big as the one he later claimed Dr Clarke had used, but as the doctor withdrew the needle he threw another spanner into the night's works.

'This will make you drowsy,' he told Sam. 'But I see you have Jim Daly with you. He can drive you home.'

The good doctor clearly knew nothing of Daly's disastrous driving record.

'S'all right,' Sam murmured, fumbling for his trousers on a floor that was rising and falling like a roller-coaster, 'I'm all . . .'

Dr Clarke caught him before he hit the floor and brought him and his trousers up together in one practised swoop. Before he could make a protest of any kind he was being half-carried out to the passenger door of the van.

'Move over, Jim,' Dr Clarke briskly ordered Daly. 'He's feeling drowsy. You'll have to drive him home.'

Most of the impact of five hot whiskeys evaporated in a flash as Daly grasped the reality of the situation. He scrambled out of the passenger seat, held the door open and kept his head well averted from the doctor.

'Goodnight, men, and safe home,' Dr Clarke called out before walking briskly back into his house and closing the door. The moon shone down on the deserted village street and Sam snoozing contentedly in the passenger seat. Daly raised his eyes to heaven and prayed.

'Holy Moses,' he whined, nearly sober and both pain and panic-stricken, 'amn't I the misfortunate being this bloody night?'

'Morning,' corrected Sam, making a fleeting visit to the land of the living. 'Home, James, and don't spare the horsepower.' He passed out again.

There are as many versions of the journey home as there are people to tell them. The chief participants in the drama have nothing to say on the matter.

Daly, racked with toothache and the beginnings of a hangover, without licence, insurance or any trace of driving skill, remains silent in case the police might take a retrospective interest in the affair. Sam could remember nothing except being wakened by a pecking sound on the windscreen. It was dawn and the van had come to rest against the hay bales in the shed. A puzzled hen was perched on the bonnet, tapping on the glass.

The Good Samaritan got out and stretched himself. His hip was a bit sore, but he was otherwise all right and the van seemed to be in one piece.

'I don't suppose you saw what happened?' he asked the hen, as she kept a beady eye on him. He formulated a new thought and expressed it for the first, though not the last time.

'There are times,' he said, 'when a friend in need can be a right nuisance.'

The hen put her head to one side and looked at him.

'You could tell,' Sam was fond of saying, 'that she thought I wasn't wise.'

10 *Pick a Pocket . . . or Two*

The Lord Chief Justice of Ireland once put his hand in his pocket for a handkerchief because, according to a researcher, he felt a sneeze coming on. The story shows that even exalted persons sneeze, just like real people, and his lordship evidently had no wish to spread diseases, which, as every schoolboy knows, are spread by sneezes. If every schoolboy knew what every schoolboy allegedly knew they'd be a wise lot indeed, but that's neither here nor there. There's bound to be some slight curiosity as to why the learned justice's handkerchief should rate a mention in history and it grieves me to relate that the piece of fabric is utterly irrelevant from an historical point of view. Unless, of course, you take into account that the incident happened a hundred and fifty years ago when hankies were less plentiful than they are now and the vast majority of people simply cast away (or disposed of on their sleeves) that which is now lovingly folded in Kleenex and, for some obscure reason, kept.

What makes the exalted man's handkerchief relevant is that when he put his hand in pocket to get it he found a foot. Not a foot of anything. Just a foot. You know, five toes, twenty-six bones, thirty-three joints and an entire dictionary of muscles, tendons, veins and what have you. The foot was the property of the Church of Ireland Archbishop. In fact it was actually attached to his Grace at the time. The historians, and I've read two of them on the subject, are annoyingly vague as to whether it was the right foot or the left. In the irritating way that historians have, they sacrifice anatomical accuracy on the altar of human whimsy. Neither do they mention whether the holy man was wearing the full complement of shoes and socks at the time. Since the barefooted, mendicant orders are a bit thin on the ground in the higher planes of Anglicanism we must assume that the foot was decently clad.

What interests me is the pocket in which the foot reposed. It must have been of very generous proportions when you think about it. I mean, we've all had the experience of rummaging in a pocket for something and finding, tucked away in a corner, some long-lost treasure like the stump of a pencil or a crumpled up pawn ticket. But a foot? And a live foot at that? How, you are asking yourself, could a foot be accommodated in a pocket without the knowledge of the pocket's owner? Especially when the owner of the foot was one of the most fidgety people that ever lived, a man who had constant trouble with his feet and who had been known to dangle them over the edge of the pulpit when preaching?

You can dismiss from your thoughts any notion of the Chief Justice sitting in shirt sleeves with his coat hanging over the back of his chair. Well brought up people didn't do that sort of thing in those days. Just thank your lucky stars you weren't up before him for the nineteenth century equivalent of parking on a double yellow line. A man who didn't know when a real live foot was in his pocket was likely to have freewheeling views on things like capital punishment.

I've never found a foot in my pocket but I did once find a hand there. It's a long story, especially when you take into consideration the ashtray that the hand was clutching at the time, so I suppose I should start at the beginning. I was, at the time, in the company of an extremely devout Welshman whom I shall call Llew because that was his name. He was leading a band of like-minded pilgrims to a great open-air exposition of the Welsh national religion, rugby. The great occasion was a Wales–Ireland match in Dublin.

Llew and his friends stopped over in Belfast for a period of spiritual preparation. This took the form of chasing girls, consuming vast quantities of beer and singing in three-part harmony of the fascinating talents of a female weightlifter from Pontardulais.

I had known Llew on his home turf and when he summoned me to the revelry I went, naturally. Well, you can't very well refuse, can you, boyo, otherwise we'll come up there and fetch you, disgrace you in front of the neighbours I shouldn't wonder, was more or less the tone of the command.

It was the custom in those days, indeed it may still be the case, for a certain class of people to purloin glasses, ashtrays and even towels from hotels. The trick was, it seems, to get complete sets of things, all emblazoned with the name of the hotel. Some hotels entered into the spirit of the thing by having their property stamped with STOLEN FROM . . . HOTEL, and no doubt making a modest adjustment to all their charges to cover the numerous occasions when customers rose to the bait.

On this occasion I was putting on my raincoat at the cloakroom when a hand came through the slit pocket – yes, it was that long ago – picked up the ashtray in which the attendant's tips were placed, gently emptied the coins on the counter and then dropped the ashtray into my pocket.

I was intrigued. I was at the time holding a side of the coat in each hand, which left me no means of steadying the room, so the appearance of a third hand which appeared to be mine interested both me and the cloakroom attendant, though for different reasons. Nothing much happened, for the whole thing was a diversionary move. A rugby fan behind me owned the hand and the whole manoeuvre was designed to distract attention while another fan got into the cloakroom and filled the pockets of another coat with stolen glasses.

The other coat belonged to a pompous gentleman who had had words with the Welshmen on the subject of their behaviour and nobody was getting away with that.

So they tracked down his coat and they filled his pockets with the hotel's glasses. In an atmosphere of counterfeit contrition they escorted him to his taxi, one of them carefully carrying the coat. They opened the taxi-door for him, they brushed imaginary specks of dust from his lapels and the coat-bearer methodically spread the coat across the back seat. They shook his hand and practically lifted and set him in the back seat. The pompous one, much mollified, travelled all of ten yards before the taxi stopped and he leaped out clutching his rear. Well he might clutch, too, for he had sat on his glass-filled coat. And serve you bloody right, too, was the verdict of the grinning Welshmen before they trooped back inside to resume singing the praises of the lady weightlifter.

That wasn't my only brush with pockets. In a recent, coatless summer I always carried my driver's licence in my shirt pocket. The only advantage I can think of that has emerged from our years of upheaval is that most of us always know where our driver's licences are. Before this they were often lost for years on end. The only people who carried them were car-less chancers trying to impress girls at dances, though I never could figure out how they coped if the girl called their bluff. My own bluff was called that summer day at a police road check, when I reached into my shirt pocket for the priceless document and found only nothingness.

At that moment, in a vision of blinding clarity, I saw my licence whirling merrily round in the washing machine. I mentioned this revelation to the policeman. He gave me a now-I've-heard-everything look and waved me on. I opted instead to turn round and go home to rescue the little blue book from a watery end. Too late. All I found was a wad of sodden paper. The photograph was intact but it had never amounted to much anyway.

In the next few days I was stopped and asked for my licence every time I turned a corner. I used to point at the ball of fluff with the photograph on top that I kept lying on the dash and, do you know, no comment was ever passed about it. The odd thing was that I hadn't been asked for my licence for months before the incident and I was only asked once after I got a replacement. I can't help thinking that the word was out about this character who washes his driver's licence, you should stop him and take a look at him, he's bound to be one of a dying breed. When I got a proper licence, like everybody else, nobody cared a toss.

You'll have noticed by now that the size of the pockets under discussion has been steadily declining. The chances are that the pocket as we know it may disappear for ever. It could be the dawn of a new age. After all, archaeologists rooting around Hadrian's Wall recently found some money and other odds and ends in a little basket-cum-handbag they identified as standard Roman legionary issue. It appears that the ancient Romans had no pockets. They also wore skirts and conquered all of the known world. If this all sounds familiar to you, just keep your ideas to yourself.

11 *Of Men and Motors*

Back in 1890, and therefore a bit before my time, there were only two cars in the entire State of Ohio. And they collided, giving us all a foretaste of the motor-car's true function. Once in a while that prophetic nugget surfaces in my mind, as, for example, I meet somebody coming the wrong way round a roundabout.

You are not supposed to meet anything as you come round a roundabout. The idea of these aids to smooth traffic flow is that everyone using them is going in the same direction. This is the theory. And, generally speaking, it's the practice.

A special mental density is called for to get on to a roundabout from the wrong direction. There's the discouraging flow of traffic from the right to contend with for a start. The crafty layout of the approach, with Keep Left signs cunningly stationed in the middle of the road and the subtle lines of their bases which nudge drivers in the right direction, should be enough to ram the point home.

You have to be really thick to get it wrong. You'd need to sit up all night practising, but every once in a while somebody pulls it off. Provided you survive the encounter, it can be an enlightening experience. It certainly makes me more observant of the foibles of my fellow-drivers.

As an example, soon after my last encounter, I saw a character edge up to the next roundabout, steering with one hand and shaving with the other. It was a battery shaver, which, I realise, takes some of the gloss off the story. A man with brush, lather and razor would really have maintained the lunatic standard set by the driver who couldn't tell left from right.

This is not to say that I wasn't impressed with the reality. It's not every day I come across, however fleetingly, a man whose lifestyle is so demanding that he must shave on the move. He certainly deserved a vehicle more in keeping with his implied worth. The clapped-out Mini he was driving could easily have detracted from his image in the eyes of a less objective observer.

Until I saw him in action, my previous best personal experience was the spectacle of a driver brushing his teeth. That was at traffic lights, I have to add, and not in the lunacy league at all.

He was in the inside lane and I was in the outside one and I wasn't sure I could believe what I was seeing until he rolled down the window to spit. He caught my eye and clearly mistook my look of fascination for one of disapproval, because he swallowed the lot, rolled up the window and stared resolutely ahead, clutching toothbrush and steering wheel with his right hand.

If he had the toothpaste in his other hand he must have had a fetching bit of piping down the left leg of his trousers as he crashed into gear and shot off. Then again, maybe not. Fellows who shave or brush their teeth while they're driving may defer dressing until they arrive wherever they're going.

I've seen it all, and so, perhaps, have you. Changing tapes, lighting pipes, reading the paper, making phone calls and falling asleep, all these activities can be seen as you drive. The one that impressed me most, from the living dangerously point of view, was lighting a pipe.

That's a two-handed job. A cigarette can be lit with one hand, unless you're using matches, and shaving, provided the razor is a battery model, is one-handed, too. As indeed is the process of changing a tape. And, of course, falling asleep needs no hands at all. The pipe is a different story. It must first be cleaned out and that calls for both hands and an assortment of gadgets. Then it has to be held still while the fuel is rammed into it and packed with just the right degree of firmness to burn evenly without going out.

It also has to be held with one hand while fanning the match over it.

'Would you light a pipe while you're driving?' I asked a pipeman of my acquaintance.

He was horrified.

'Certainly not,' he said, 'I always get mine going well before I leave the house.'

'And if it should go out while you're driving?' I probed.

'I keep a packet of cigarettes on the dash,' he told me, 'and I'd light one at the traffic lights.'

See what I mean? Some drivers just have a death wish, one way or another.

It takes different forms. There's the wee man who only comes out on Saturdays, for example, especially coming up to Christmas and when the sales are on. He wears a tan car coat with imitation leather piping and favours a Russian-style hat, a Paisley-pattern scarf and a pair of fur-lined gloves he got last Christmas.

He looks at the world through glasses hewn from sawn-off tumblers and finds it all a bit of a mystery, judging by what can be seen of his face after the glasses and the scarf are taken into account. He's always accompanied by a female version of himself, identical even to the glasses, but while he looks merely baffled, a downturn at the corner of her mouth suggests that you tangle with her at your peril.

They have a Morris Minor, or something of similar vintage, held together with polish and tender, loving care. The seats are covered with a furry material and a toy noddy dog squats forever on their rear window shelf, guarding them from all harm and obscuring their vision. Sometimes the furry dog is replaced by a pair of furry dice, which is more symbolic, because, if they would only but realise it, this well-matched pair are dicing with death.

They are to be found in the queue for a busy carpark. Not on the right hand side of the road, nor even on the left, but diagonally across the white line. Behind them and towering over them is a lorry that is not trying to get into the car park. It contains ten tons of bricks for a city centre building site and the wee man is holding up delivery.

He is also denying the use of the road to a busload of shoppers from the County Limerick approaching from the opposite direction. Behind both bus and lorry a traffic queue has formed and the honking of the frustrated driver is heard in the land.

The wee man is mystified by all the noise. He looks at her. She looks at him. They resume staring straight ahead. She appears to be putting a curse on the right headlamp of the shoppers' coach. He is similarly engaged with the left one. The effect is heightened by the occasional glint of wintry sun on the sawn-off tumblers.

The orderly queue for the car park, neatly lined along the left hand kerb, suddenly wakens to the presence of a motionless line of through traffic hiding the entrance from them. For all they know somebody may have sneaked in ahead of them. Mutiny breaks out on low key stuff at first. Just a bit of horn-blowing, then wives and children start spilling out of the cars, the wives hurling instructions over their shoulders about when, where – and if – the family will ever be united again.

The driver of the brick lorry leans his right elbow on the steering wheel, cups his cheek in hand and settles down to read the paper he keeps on the passenger seat for just such emergencies. He doesn't mind if the queue honks horns till doomsday, it's nothing to do with him. He's not blocking the road. Their vision may be, but not the road. Even if the drivers behind think he's responsible, none among them will climb the step to his cab and tell him to move on.

The coach driver and his charges watch this curious Northern ritual with courteous detachment. No horn-blowing, light-flashing or other provocative gesture of disapproval emanates from their vehicle. Dem Nordeners are mad enough for anything, you can almost hear them thinking.

Then a man laden with parcels and accompanied by a small boy arrives on the scene. They have no idea how closely their every move is studied. Their car is clearly visible to virtually the whole traffic jam. Daddy puts his parcels on the roof of his car and begins to rummage for his keys. Please, God, prays the assembled multitude, surely you didn't let the eejit lose his keys? He hasn't lost them but he has entrusted them to his offspring who chooses that moment to be coy and hide among the cars from his dear Daddy.

There is a brief outbreak of hide and seek, then Junior decides to surrender. Now it's only a matter of searching every pocket for the ticket. By the time Daddy has found it, fished out the right change, stowed offspring and parcels, everybody except the wee man and his wife have aged visibly.

Father and son depart, the driver nearest the entrance yields the right of way and Tweedledum and Tweedledee chug in leisurely fashion into the solitary empty space.

The brick lorry, the coach and their retinues are galvanised into life. The rest of the queue give up and follow them. The wee man and his wife emerge from the carpark. She is wearing boots designed for trekking across Siberia and she has a handbag big enough to carry him.

'Traffic's heavy today,' he says.

'Shakkin,' she agrees, without unlocking her teeth.

'I know your wee man,' a lorry driver said to me one time, 'or maybe it was his first cousin. He used to have a lovely wee Ford.'

'That "used to have" sounds a bit ominous,' I remarked. 'How do you know so much about it?'

'Oh,' said the lorry driver, 'he came out of hibernation last Spring and I spotted him on the Shore Road. He was tootling down the white line at fifteen miles an hour and I was right behind him. That car was a real dazzler. Twenty years old if it was a day but it looked better than new. He must have spent his whole life polishing it.'

'The "used to" bit is what I want to hear about,' I prompted.

'Ah, well, he was going so slow I didn't notice when he stopped. I ran into the back of him and both doors fell off at the same time. It was like something out of a cartoon,' was the driver's response.

'Then what?' I asked.

'I gave him a hand to carry the bits and pieces over to the side,' the lorry driver told me. 'It was just as you say, there was nothing holding it together but the polish.'

'What did he say?'

The lorry driver looked embarrassed.

'Nothing,' he told me. 'He just stood there and cried.'

'Lucky for you his wife wasn't there,' was my comment. 'You'd have been crying, too.'

Bits fall off cars even without a clout from a lorry. The speed with which they're replaced is in direct proportion to their relevance in keeping the machine moving.

A wheel has to be replaced almost immediately, for example, although punctures needn't be repaired at all if someone else is driving your car. It's doubtful if those pieces of exhaust pipe you see littering the roads every day are ever replaced. Certainly not on the motors you hear careering round in the wee small hours of the morning.

On the other hand, horns never seem to break down or fall off. Windscreen wipers fall into an in-between category, as do petrol caps. Several times during my motoring career I have lost wipers and have done like everyone else. If it came off the driver's side I just borrowed the one from the passenger side. If it was lost from the passenger side in the first place there's no great hurry in replacing it anyway.

Herself has once or twice expressed disapproval of this cavalier attitude, on the grounds that she can't see where she's going. Blithe quips from me that whither I go she goeth also cut remarkably little ice, for some reason.

I had a screw-on petrol cap once that I had been meaning to replace for about a year and a half when the decision was taken out of my hands by an assortment of vandals in Sligo. They took my wipers, though I retrieved one from a nearby cemetery, and they took the petrol cap as well. They replaced it with a box of matches which they tried to light but a kindly deity intervened and decreed that the Kellymobile should survive and creak along for another while.

While all this was taking place I was sound asleep in a nearby guesthouse and didn't realise the full horror of my near-predicament until the next morning. There may be worse fates than standing beside the burnt-out wreckage of your pride and joy on a wet Sunday morning, on the Sligo to Enniskillen road, but at that moment I couldn't think of one. It would have been no sort of reward for a car that had beaten planned obsolesence and survived the repayments as well.

Since the net loss was one petrol cap and one wiper I got off lightly enough and I gained something as well. I gained from the landlady the priceless opinion that it was probably done because the car had a Northern registration.

I have never unravelled the political/mechanical/geographical niceties of that remark but it has certainly given me something to think about on the long nights when there's nothing much on television.

It was no problem replacing the wiper the next day but a lockable petrol cap (a perfect case of locking the stable door after the horsepower almost bolted) proved to be more difficult. I visited most of the spare parts centres, only to be told in each case my best plan was to go to the agents.

Uninvolved persons may well ask why I hadn't done this in the first place but I had a good reason for not so doing and thrawness had much to do with it. Before the petrol cap incident, in fact for a long time before it, there had been another bit of the Kellymobile missing. Nothing vital, just the button that locks or unlocks the driver's door from the inside. It wasn't all missing, actually, just the bit that stuck above the level of the door and I broke it by the simple expedient of catching it in the seat belt as I opened the door.

Nothing urgent, as you can see. Once in a while I would remember to mention it to somebody and after a month or two I had a collection of buttons, none of which fitted but I kept them anyway. It would have been ungrateful to so many obliging souls, who had taken the trouble to remember what I kept forgetting, not to store them in a safe place.

One day the inevitable happened and the whole mechanism jammed on the underside of the panel. I began a pilgrimage round the spare parts shops, only to be met with the repetitious cry, 'You'd be better to go to the agents.'

I repaired thither. The spares counter was under the command of one Jobsworth. 'That's more than me job's worth, mister' is the motto on his family coat-of-arms.

I described my problem to him and he listened with some irritation.

'Now if you'd only come in yesterday,' he said, 'it would have been no problem.'

'You mean you have none?' I asked. 'You sold the last one this morning?'

'We've never sold any at all,' was his reply. 'Those things never break.'

I didn't much like the suggestion that I was setting some kind of record for mechanical ineptitude but I let it pass without comment.

'We had a half a gross gathering dust in the stores until yesterday,' he went on, glowering at me. 'Now they're parcelled up over there, ready to go back to England this afternoon. The paperwork's all done and the carton's sealed with metal bands. Did you think of taking a look round a breaker's yard?'

By way of a parable I told him about the time my starter broke in Donegal. I went to the local garage, run by a couple of lads with oil on their faces. They dismantled the starter and showed me its mangled innards. Then they told me they had one just in for a local farmer, but sure he was baling hay and could do without for a day or two till they could get him another one from Derry. And I drove off half an hour later with his starter in my car.

Jobsworth said, a trifle impatiently, that he couldn't see the point. I put it to him another way. I said it would be a long, cold, hard, frosty day in a certain hot place before I troubled him again. Which is why I didn't go to him for the petrol cap.

I got a locking petrol cap in another place, the last one on my list, but they had to guess the price for they'd never been asked for one for my type of car before, but they kept the one just in case.

As you can see, my motoring experiences have all been out of the ordinary.

12 *The Fortunes of Bungalow Magill*

Bungalow Magill is no longer with us but when he was, his sliding door gear caused him endless bother. He was a martyr to it, and his curious affliction was a puzzle to many, for when he was badly afflicted he would screw up his face in the weirdest contortions, point to his shoes and use words that made winos blanch and move to the other side of the street. It was all quite simple, really. He had an ingrowing toenail. Or, to use the curious upside down language that Bungalow had made his own, he had an intoeing grow-nail.

He had, it seems, been sufficiently moved on one never-to-be-forgotten occasion to take his problem to the hospital. In a spirit of curiosity he had asked the doctor who treated him the cause of his nail problem and the doctor, casting around for an image that would be comprehensible to Bungalow, told him that his nail grew in a groove similar to that in which a sliding door moved. He based this figure of speech on the assumption that Bungalow was a joiner. The worthy Bungalow did not disabuse him of this notion, although he was no more a joiner than he was a meteorologist. He was in fact about as handless and footless as it was possible to get without falling.

From that day on, however, Bungalow made medical history. Not simply because of the nail, but because the doctor had also mentioned the presence of a wart on the sole of his foot. Thus Bungalow had a farouk to keep his inadequate cabinet-fittings company in his overcrowded shoe. The defunct Egyptian monarch certainly came down in the world when he made the acquaintance of Bungalow's socks.

'You're limping,' we used to say to him sympathetically.

'Och, the slidin' door tackle's wrecked again,' he would say, employing words that could never be printed. 'And the farouk's givin' me hell, too.'

He claimed to be from Cookstown, although it could never be proved.

'He would tell YOU that,' an acquaintance said to me once in tones that suggested that I had been created and placed in this world to be lied to. I let the slur pass. Anyway, why should anyone bother to tell me lies?

Some people held that he came from a village near Omagh, and further alleged, which I can very well believe, that he had been a sore tribulation to his family and his neighbours. Nobody was ever specific about the form his rascality took but he lived in a more self-righteous era, when to be a bit unorthodox was viewed as evidence of criminal tendencies. At some stage, much to the relief of the locality, he decided to emigrate to America and everybody rose magnificently to the occasion. A massive send-off was organised, and, as was the custom of the time and place, a whipround was set in motion to ensure him, if not a good start in the New World, at least his departure from the Old.

He went, too, but only as far as Omagh. Here he fell among evil companions and they all indulged freely in the electric soup till the money was done. After three days Bungalow reappeared in his hometown, drunk as a lord and enquiring in an American accent the way to his father's house. There was no fatted calf, however, although his mother is supposed to have rained a few blows of a sweeping brush on his head for the disgrace he had brought on them.

Bungalow had enough wit to know that the days of wine and roses had come to an end, so he took himself to Belfast and embraced the profession of builder's labourer.

That was the designation that usually appeared on the charge sheet but the truth was that no builder in his right mind would have had him anywhere near him, for he was inseparable from trouble. He worked, if that is the correct expression, for a house-repairer. Any time I saw him engaged in this activity, he was leaning against a wall, usually not the one being repaired, smoking and whistling after the girls. I use the term 'girls' loosely. If they were female and mobile they qualified for Bungalow's ear-splitting attentions. The whistling was all the more piercing because of the peculiar arrangement of his front teeth.

The whistling cost him his job in the house-repair business. His employer was renovating a house facing a butcher's shop and Bungalow was assisting him, mainly by loafing and smoking. And, of course, whistling. It was a lengthy business – house-repairing always is – and the whistling had become no more than a background noise, except to the butcher's assistant. This lad fancied the wee girl in the home bakery and he advised Bungalow to refrain from paying his noisy attentions.

Now Bungalow, it must be said, was not a man of violence. When he advised the young man about where to go and what to do with himself when he got there, he was speaking in a purely figurative manner. That, however, was not how the lad saw it. There was only one blow struck and it went some way to rearranging Bungalow's dental oddities. That was not the end of the matter, not by a long chalk, not as far as Bungalow was concerned.

It was the young butcher's first duty every morning to wash down the shop window, a task he always finished by throwing the remaining soapy water all over the glass.

Under the guise of making peace the morning after the punch-up, Bungalow managed to drop a brick he just happened to have handy into the bucket. Within seconds the shop had no window and the stock on display was tastefully decorated with broken glass, with the mortar-covered brick as centrepiece.

It was the most exciting day that street ever saw. Bungalow's boss had a hangover, an invalid horse had trotted off with most of his money the previous afternoon and he and his wife were not on speaking terms. He was aching for a row with somebody and the angry butcher filled the bill nicely. Right and wrong didn't come into it, not at the start anyway. It was the two builders versus the two butchers and a full and frank exchange of views took place, mainly concerning the parentage of each side. They didn't actually come to close quarters, for the builders knew that the butchers had an unholy expertise with a variety of lethal instruments.

The dust settled eventually and Bungalow was just beginning to see his employer in a new light when he got the sack. Well, there was the matter of the broken window, Bungalow's general uselessness and the unnatural excitement he generated wherever he went to be taken into account. Whatever bad language the builder hadn't used up on the butcher he poured out on his assistant.

'The language was fearful,' Bungalow said afterwards, seemingly unaware of his own contribution to the cultural enrichment of the area. 'He was the most ignorant man I ever met. He was as ignorant as a pig packin' china.'

A master of the memorable phrase was Bungalow.

He subsequently spent several hours in the painting and decorating trade. He was brought by his new employer to a house in a prosperous suburb and set to stripping wallpaper.

The boss made the mistake of going away and leaving him to it. The lady of the house had a mortal dread of being cheated by workmen and she kept coming in to see that Bungalow was keeping his back bent. At one point her stealthy entrance went badly wrong, the door caught the worker's elbow and did some damage to the inaptly named funny-bone.

Bungalow retaliated as only he could and the shaken householder retreated to the phone, screaming that she had never, ever, been spoken to in such a manner before. She gave a word by word account of the affair to the boss, but by then the culprit had left the premises. Before he went, however, he opened a tin of paint and added a comment about the customer in letters a foot high.

When challenged about this he asserted that she had done it herself to blacken his character. He himself couldn't write, he said.

He had been able to once but the gift had been mysteriously taken from him one night as he slept.

It was at this time that I lost track of him, although I did hear later that he had become involved in the greyhound industry, to the extent of actually owning a greyhound. This was hotly denied by one owner.

'It was no greyhound,' he said crossly. 'It was just some sort of a long dog.'

Bungalow's name cropped up in conversation recently and I remembered to ask the question that has been bothering me for years.

'Why' I asked, 'was he called Bungalow?'

'Because he had nothing upstairs,' I was told.

Well, I don't know. I'm sure he was the man who sold a dead greyhound – or maybe it was just a long dog – to a punter at Dundalk Stadium. Of course, that's another story.

13 *Counter Attack*

Herself has pointed out to me more than once that I'm no great shakes at the shopping. There's some truth in this. I tend to buy the first thing that looks remotely suitable for my purpose, pay what I'm asked and stuff the change in my pocket without a second look.

I do have misgivings about this method from time to time. In some shops it can be damaging to the financial well-being to buy more than two items at once. This is because nobody can use the cash register. The assistant takes your fiver or your tenner, tilts her eyes to a peculiar angle, does the calculations in her head and rings up the total. The human head is not a reliable place in which to do calculations that involve somebody else's money. A stump of a pencil and the back of an envelope are more reliable. Well, marginally.

I occasionally wonder, though I've never had the nerve to ask, why shops of this sort bother to spend huge sums on elaborate machines that could practically make the tea for you and yet are used only as cash-boxes. Or why, for that matter, they bother to employ people who can't use them? Of course I appreciate that there are wheels within wheels and jobs must be found for the more inept of the family connection . . . or else, possibly.

There are snags to be encountered, I'll admit, when the assistant actually knows how the machine works. A palsied finger, still affected by the ravages of the night before, may easily hit a wrong button or two and the total arrived at may be a mere approximation.

Another source of concern to me is pricing. I have a deep, possibly primitive, distrust of articles that aren't priced. In the good old days, whatever they were, some shops, especially in the drapery trade, used a coding system. It was based on some arbitrary selection of letters, like the owner's grandmother's maiden name, or other secret formula.

The system was so bewildering that it was an immediate hit with those demented people who used to formulate Eleven Plus questions . . . enough to condemn it for all eternity.

The customer, of course, hadn't a clue about what anything cost. The shopkeeper did, though, and so did his assistants, and they could rattle off the dreadful truth with such an infuriating air of superiority that the customer assumed the prices were made up on the spot. And, of course, tailored to whatever degree of wealth or gullibility he displayed.

Matters have now entered a different dimension, especially in supermarkets. The customer is still kept in the dark, and the IQ of the assistant is irrelevant, for all she has to do is pass the purchase over a species of eye in the cash register and the price pops up on the display. It even tells the assistant how much change is due.

This is a chilling development. The day is drawing even nearer when computer shall speak unto computer and humanity will finally become irrelevant.

There's no one so irrelevant as the solitary customer trying to muscle in on a group of sales staff discussing their social lives. It was hinted to me one time that one of the family would like a purse for her birthday and it was further implied that a quality item was what was sought. I took all this subtlety on board, as they say, and entered a downtown store where purses of a suitable standard were plentiful, as indeed were the staff, because there were four of them and I was the only customer. There was, in addition, a management-type person who managed to both smile mechanically and ignore me each time he passed. A useful trick that, and an essential element in retail management training courses, or so it seems to me from time to time.

I finally cajoled a reluctant assistant away from her coven and mentioned not just my errand but the fact that none of the purses had a price marked on it. She knew nothing of these mundane matters either but she was not entirely devoid of initiative. Each one I selected was held up and the remainder of the coven were invited to submit quotations. All my ancient, peasant suspicions about arbitrary pricing surfaced, for although none of the other three could agree on a price for any one purse, the minimum began to sound like the ground rent bill for the shop.

I excused myself as civilly as I could and completed my transaction in another shop where everything was clearly marked, because they apparently didn't subscribe to the notion that if you've got to ask the price you can't afford to shop here.

Even so, I stuffed the change into my pocket in man-of-the-world fashion, for that's another of my ancient hang-ups. It dates from a day in the distant past when a customer in front of me told the assistant she had given him a pound too much change. She smiled sweetly, thanked him profusely and dropped the pound back into the till. He wasn't even out of earshot when she turned to me and spoke.

'I hate people who check their change,' she told me.

That experience made me cautious. You see, I can recall the venom in her voice as freshly and vibrantly as if it were yesterday.

As an indifferent shopper I never cease to be amazed at the

variety of gimmickry – catchpennies, an older generation would have called them – available to the spending public. Some items, of course, are designed to be bought as presents and have no other discernible function to the uninitiated.

I can well remember my bafflement the first time I saw an electric toothbrush. It looked somehow familiar but I couldn't quite identify its role in the scheme of things, so I asked, being a firm believe that if ye ask, ye shall receive, even if what ye receive is only abuse.

'It's an electric toothbrush,' I was informed crisply, as if such a thing was the most natural development in the world.

'Well, goodness, gracious me,' I remarked, or words to that effect, 'do you mean to tell me that the age of the electric tooth has arrived? Isn't evolution just too amazing.'

An electric toothbrush, I soon learned, is no joking matter, especially when it's the gift of a thoughtful girlfriend to the joker's son.

I still think that some people have more money than wit, but while that's a criticism, in the retail trade it's money from America.

Since the memorable day when the electric toothbrush entered my experience I have come to know several other people who drive them. I also know a man who is totally hooked on Chinese poetry of the fifth century – in translation, let me add, by way of expiation – and another who is adamant that the Earth is flat and that all the pictures allegedly transmitted from the moon in fact emanate from Tibet. I'm not bragging about my oddball acquaintances, just making the point that all told they outnumber the users of electric toothbrushes.

These users are enthusiastic about the merits of their sophisticated appliances. They save time, they insist, which is a considerable bonus since they came free in the first place.

'And what do you do with the time you save?' is a question I have been known to ask, because I come from the Sperrins, which is a thing I may have mentioned before, and that sort of practical information is much prized in those parts. I ask as a sort of reflex, you understand, for like most information it would be completely useless even if I got it.

Herself often wonders how I've lived so long unscathed. I say it's because I've been touched by the hand of Allah, and in proof of this assertion I occasionally produce my favourite possession. It's a photograph showing me standing in the oldest mosque in all Islam, facing Mecca in the manner prescribed by the Koran. She remains unconvinced.

Electric toothbrushes were nothing to the culture shock I experienced when I was first shown an electric shoebrush. It was shown to me by the manager of an electrical shop because it worried him, he said, to see people going out of his establishment with money still in their possession. It bothered him so much, he further claimed, that he had trained his staff specially to take anybody's cash.

If the electric toothbrush gave me something to think about, the wonder of the electric shoe-polishing brush really knocked me sideways.

'Do you know what I've just seen?' I asked a colleague on the never-to-be-forgotten day I experienced this culture shock. 'An electric shoe-polishing brush. Did you ever hear the like of it?'

She had. Not, in fact, an electric gadget, something far better. She settled back and told me the sad tale of the family in what passes for the stockbroker belt in these parts. There was a Mammy and a Daddy, and there were two daughters and a son. There was also The Help. But hard times came a-knocking on the door and sacrifices had to be made. The Help – they were plural – were sacrificed first. Not literally, you understand, they were merely sacked and the chores formerly carried out by the underlings were reallocated. To the daughters.

Now the girls had their own jobs to go to, so their new domestic duties had to be fitted in before they went out and after they came home. To one was formally allocated the task of polishing their brother's shoes. He was fit and possessed the normal number of hands as well as feet to place in the shoes that other hands had polished.

I remarked that it was a pity that we hadn't known about the electric polishing gadget in time, for the pair of us could have clubbed up and bought him one. My remark floated away in stony silence, for my colleague's eyes were glazed over. In her mind I fancy she saw the tumbrels rattling over the cobblestones and Madame Defarge selling ice-cream below the guillotine. And who could blame her? Heads have rolled for far less down the ages.

None of the foregoing should be taken to mean that I'm implacably hostile to gadgets. I possess one that I simply knew I had to own the minute I saw it.

It's two feet long and looks remarkably like a skinny, flexible hypodermic needle, with a plunger and grip at one end. When you press the plunger four little spring-loaded, L-shaped pieces of metal leap out of the business end at right angles to each other. Release the plunger and they shoot right back in again. I was fascinated.

'What's it for?' I asked the assistant.

She wasn't sure but she thought about it.

'I believe,' she answered carefully, 'that mechanics use them for fishing up screws and things that fall down the sides of engines.'

I have never dropped a screw down the sides of my car engine, because its workings are a mystery to me and I leave them to mechanics to probe. It's bad enough to observe them shake their heads dolefully and suck in their breath when there's no provocation involved. Evidence of interference by amateurs could put the bill through the roof.

The bill for the gadget was small. It was made by the industrious citizens of Taiwan whose cost-effective production techniques and low wages made it possible to market the appliance for fifty pence. It had neither name nor operating instructions but for fifty pence you can't have everything. I bought it in a large department store near Cloughmills on a day when it was raining heavily between the showers, and as the sales assistant tried in vain to make it stay in a plastic bag, Herself appeared like a genie out of a bottle. She had been frustrated in the fashion department.

'What's that?' she demanded suspiciously.

'I don't know,' I told her. For once the paths of truth and cowardice coincided. I had no idea what the thing might be useful for.

Inspiration came from that evening's paper. Someone, somewhere in Ireland, using primitive equipment, had discovered treasure. And I knew where unclaimed treasure lurked. Down the sides of our settee there was wealth untold but the gap was too tight for my fingers. I could locate objects but not grip them.

I got to work and I have to confess that the initial results were unpromising. The first thing to emerge was a tiny egg-shaped article, cracked all over its surface. In science fiction movies these things always hatch out monsters that bite you on the leg and make off with the family pet. This item contained nothing more interesting than a nut. Herself found this symbolic.

The next item to surface was a defunct ball-point, commercial value nil. Two crisps followed, then a wine gum and a small, formerly white object stamped Mint, which proved on closer inspection to be made of rubber.

This discovery cost me my audience, which departed in a cloud of derision. Just as well, too, for the gadget next emerged clutching a shiny 20 pence piece. I was elated. I was only 30 pence down.

Then I really hit paydirt. The thing emerged clutching a pound coin in its tiny metal jaws. There was a greenish stain along one edge, it's true, but it was legal tender and it was all mine, mine, I tell you. From there on everything was profit, I told myself.

Returns actually lessened from that point. A sweet in a wrapper and four pieces of silver paper brought the vein to an end. Still, they testified to my mastery of The Gadget. It was time, metaphorically, to load up the burro and move on.

The armchairs proved disappointing. A single-bladed penknife and a five peseta piece were hardly a high enough yield for me to go public.

Exploration of the car's handbrake housing was more encouraging. The Gadget came up clutching a fifty pence piece. Also a screw which possibly belonged down there though I fervently hoped not. Still, I'd made £1.20 on the deal and not everybody who goes into a Cloughmills department store on a day when it's raining heavily between the showers can say that much.

14 *Larry's Game*

The trouble with me, Donovan used to say, is that I have a conscience. He would deliver the news of this affliction in pretty much the same tones he might have used to express a preference for a particular brand of cornflakes. And that, let me add, would have been a more obvious phenomenon than the promptings of his still, small voice.

His conscience only surfaced, in my experience of him anyway, when he missed out on the chance to get involved in a dubious enterprise, or when he had been rebuffed by some female or other. It was then that he adopted his high moral tone and gave off, in pious vein, about the way society was crumbling at the edges.

At times like these he would express grave doubts about what would happen to the planet when the next generation got their hands on it. He would shake his head sadly at the demise of loyalty, in the case of the dubious enterprise, or of good taste in the case of the unimpressed female, and order another round.

His conscience was a purely night-time matter, I told him once, and I challenged him to prove that it ever caused him any problems in daylight. He was hurt, he told me. He wanted me to know that he was a fully committed, 25 hours a day, eight days a week, morally upright citizen. In support of this astounding revelation he told me the story of Larry the barman.

Donovan was employed, theoretically at any rate, by a company building a large housing development at the time of his story, and it was the company's practice to send transport to pick up their employees from various points. Donovan's pick-up point was a nearby roundabout and it was his habit to set off from his digs half-an-hour beforehand, so as to be in good time.

This was nonsense. Time meant practically nothing to him. If he got the day right he regarded that as the height of punctuality. But I let it pass, except to mention that people out and about as early as he claimed hadn't been home all night or just had bad consciences. He glowered at the reference to conscience and rambled on.

It was his hobby at the time, he claimed, to study the design of houses that he passed, so as to form some idea of the kind of place he would build for himself when he finally amassed enough money to do it. In view of his unending generosity towards the support of three-legged horses and ailing greyhounds, it was an ambition unlikely to be fulfilled.

From his perch on the roundabout he had a particularly good view of one house and to listen to him you would think it was some millionaire's weekend place. The lawns were razored. There was a double garage, extended upwards and outwards. There was a set of garden furniture with a striped umbrella over the table. I waited in vain for details of kitchen fittings and gold bathroom taps. He knew of old when he had stretched the limits of my credibility.

On the way home in the evenings he didn't get off at the roundabout but at a pub half a mile farther down the road. He always called in, he told me, and had just the one pint. This was to emphasise his abstemious character. Since he could down three or four pints absent-mindedly in the course of telling any given yarn, I nodded my connivance at this fiction too.

Then one evening the barman remarked that he was unusually quiet. Any silence emanating from Donovan's direction was worthy of remark.

'I was thinking about a house,' he told the barman, one Larry by name.

'Is that all?' said Larry, who plainly thought there were more interesting things to think about, but then he was only a young fellow.

'It's a great bungalow,' Donovan said, 'and the view is terrific. It's near the roundabout. And the lawns, you'd think they'd been trimmed with a razor.'

'Oh, it's a good house all right,' said Larry, polishing away at the glasses.

'Double garage and all,' Donovan went on wistfully, 'He must be well-heeled, that fella. I wonder how many bedrooms it has?'

'Four,' said Larry, still polishing away.

'Four,' Donovan repeated, 'Four. How do you know?'

'It's mine,' said Larry.

'Get away,' snorted Donovan.

'It's true,' said Larry. 'It's mine.'

'You married money?' Donovan queried.

'I did not,' said Larry indignantly,' She hadn't a penny of her own.'

'Well, then,' probed Donovan, 'she must have a great job?'

'She's a full-time housewife,' the barman told him.

Donovan went home in a thoroughly confused state of mind. The more he thought about it, the more a great truth began to reveal itself. He was in the wrong line of work and on the wrong side of the bar.

He told the whole story to a workmate the next day. He heard him out, tapped the side of his nose knowingly, tucked an imaginary violin under his chin and drew an invisible bow across it.

'Do you mean what I think you mean?' Donovan asked him, and I visualised the sanctimonious look that must have crossed his face at that moment.

'Certainly,' said the other man. 'He's fiddling. Bound to be.'

'Well,' said Donovan to me, 'I couldn't let it go on. The boss of that place was being robbed blind. My conscience wouldn't let me stand idly by.'

Even long after the event he was still carried away by his own piety.

Righting the wrong proved to be difficult. Every evening when he came in Larry was in charge. In fact Donovan had never seen anyone but Larry behind the bar all the time he had been coming into the place. One day, however, fortune smiled.

It was about a fortnight after the conversation with Larry that he found an elderly gent behind the bar. He was dignified, portly and he had a gold watch-chain across his middle. He exuded authority and prosperity.

'Are you the boss?' Donovan asked him.

'When Larry's not here,' said the man, with what Donovan took to be a trace of sarcasm.

Donovan took a reflective sip or two of his pint.

'Have you ever seen that bungalow of his?' he asked eventually.

'No,' said the other man, 'What about it?'

Donovan broke into lyrical detail about the bungalow and its location, its four bedrooms, manicured lawns, its double garage and the garden umbrella that didn't advertise anything.

'You're not going to tell me,' he said, 'that a young fellow like him could do all that on a barman's wages?'

'You're right,' said the older man, 'not on a barman's wages. I don't see how it could be done.'

'Well,' said Donovan, 'What are you going to do about it?'

'Nothing,' was the response, 'not a thing.'

Donovan was shocked by this indifference.

'You should get rid of him,' he told the portly man behind the bar. 'No messing, just get rid of him.'

'Ah, no,' said the man, 'sure the next fellow would only have to get a four-bedroomed bungalow with a double garage and a striped umbrella for the garden. Where would it all end?'

Donovan's involvement ended at this point. He had done his bit to right the wrong and his conscience was clear. He didn't know what the world was coming to, he assured me, when a man would have to stand by and be robbed blind, simply because the devil he knew was preferable to one he didn't.

He never went back to the bar after that but his conscience had nothing to do with that development. The very next day he had offered to bend a shovel over the foreman's head and had got the sack. It was this tendency to physical violence that kept me from telling him it was a small world and that I knew the hostelry in question.

Larry was well entitled to his comfortable bungalow, if that was what he chose to spend his money on. In the upside down way of the world it was the portly and distinguished gentleman who was the barman and young Larry was the owner.

There's a time and a place for everything but Donovan in pious mood would never be receptive to suggestions that jumping to conclusions is an inadequate form of exercise for mind or body.

I'll tell him eventually.

15 *Catnapping*

I'll call him Tom. It's not his real name, but sure, what's in a name anyway? He's a fidgety, restless sort of a fellow, the kind that never knows what to do with himself on a day off, which is a thing that's a sore tribulation to his wife, his family and his acquaintances.

This particular Saturday he was hanging around the house, peering into cupboards, walking up and down the hall, out into the garden and generally getting under her feet. So she hastily devised a number of messages he might do for her down at the local shopping centre and sent him off. That way she thought she might get a few minutes peace. Maybe, with luck, an hour.

He was driving down the street when he spotted an elderly neighbour standing at her gate in a state of distress. Full of concern, he drew up alongside.

'What's the matter, Mrs Smith?' he asked.

'It's my cat,' she said. 'Look.'

He got out and looked. The cat was dead. Unquestionably dead. Its nine lives had run out. And so, it would appear, had the cat, right under the wheels of a passing vehicle.

'Don't worry about it,' he told her. 'I'm sure it was all over quickly. I'm sure it felt nothing.'

The demise of the cat, it turned out, had nothing to do with her distress.

'What am I to do with that?' she demanded crossly, and she pointed to the mangled corpse. Disposal of the remains rather than the demise of the cat preocuppied this down-to-earth animal-lover.

'It's no problem,' said Tom gallantly. 'If you would get me a plastic bag, and a brush and shovel . . .'

The old dear trotted off and was back in a flash with the brush, the shovel, a sheet of crumpled tissue paper and a plastic bag. The plastic bag was to be crucial to the events of the rest of the morning. It was a Harrods' bag, and to some people that is no inconsiderable status symbol.

The old lady stood at a discreet distance while he scooped up the mortal remains and shovelled them onto the tissue paper. He rolled up the tissue paper, put it in the Harrods' bag, assured the old lady that he would dispose of the package as soon as he got home. Then he placed the bag on the passenger seat and went on about his business.

The events of the day might have taken a completely different turn if he had done a couple of things the police are forever encouraging motorists to do. He should have put the Harrods' bag out of sight and he should have locked the car but he did neither. It was only when he came out of the supermarket some time later that he realised he might have put temptation in the path of the evilly disposed, for a well-dressed woman was standing by the passenger door and looking furtively around.

Then, right before his astonished eyes, she whipped open the door, grabbed the Harrods' bag and made for the car-park exit like the proverbial scalded cat.

At first he stood and stared, overcome by the brazen hilarity of the thing, but then a dreadful curiosity seized him, so he hastily stowed the shopping in the boot and followed at a respectable distance.

There was a bus-stop close to the car-park exit and that's where he found her. She stood languidly in a queue of three, the very model of a person who would shop in Harrods. The other two were substantial citizens, too, wearing His and Her sheepskin coats, fur hats and propped up on matching umbrellas. It was a typical suburban Saturday autumn scene.

Tom loitered for a moment or two, unsure of what to do next. There didn't seem much point in accosting the well-dressed thief and demanding the return of a stolen dead cat, but some whimsical force held him there.

The bus was slow in coming, the way buses often are, and the sheepskin-coated pair's desultory conversation become more animated. The thief looked cautiously around, slipped her hand into the bag and her face lit up. The situation was suddenly bright with possibilities and Tom watched with interest.

She continued to rummage among the tissue paper, then she took another furtive look around, peered into the bag, screamed and collapsed on the pavement in a dead faint.

At this point the two in the matching sheepskins began to shout instructions to each other, collide, jump up and down and generally behave as people do in this kind of emergency. As a piece of entertainment Tom thought it couldn't have been bettered.

It could. Just when the excitement was at its height the deity who presides over these debacles took a hand and sent an ambulance along the road. The male of the sheepskin-coated pair jumped out waving his furled umbrella and imploring it to stop. It did, the ambulance-men produced a stretcher, placed the catnapper carefully on it and were just about to drive off when the female of the pair began to hammer on the door with one hand while she held up the Harrods' bag in the other.

An ambulance man dismounted, opened the back door and solemnly placed the bag on the still-unconscious bag-snatcher's stomach.

Tom doesn't know what happened next. His dearest wish, he often says, would have been to be a fly on the wall when the light-fingered lady was brought into casualty, clutching the mangled remains of a stolen cat. He would love to know what was written in the hospital report. He would like to have heard her explanation, if one was possible.

He says he wishes he had had the presence of mind to race back to the car park, get his car and follow the ambulance to casualty, but Belfast has several hospitals and she might have been taken to any of them. And anyway it's just as well he didn't follow.

He's the kind of man who brings disaster in his wake. As he walks along the street, his friends say, the air is full of the sound of things falling out of their ordained places as his shadow falls on them. He's the last person a busy casualty department needs on a Saturday afternoon.

16 *Children, Seen and Heard*

A friend of mine went into a crowded eating place one lunch-time and ordered lasagne. He regretted the decision as soon as it was placed in front of him, because the stuff on the plate bore only the faintest resemblance to what he thought he had ordered.

Time was short and he was hungry, so he struggled with it and hoped for the best. About halfway through his repast he was joined by a woman and a lad of about ten. It's usual in these circumstances for the newcomers to say things like 'Do you mind if we sit here?' even if the question is purely rhetorical and the answer ignored.

No such courtesies were offered. The lad, he told me later, was a sullen-looking lump, an affliction he assumed he inherited from his mother. This conclusion was based on hindsight.

Mammy asked her offspring what he wanted to eat. The offspring first scowled at my friend, then at the lasagne and concluded this survey by sticking his finger into it. To add insult to injury he licked the finger.

'I want that,' he snarled to his mother.

Well, of course, she was outraged.

'Robert,' she said severely, for such was the revolting brat's name, 'you don't like that stuff. Have something else.'

'Chips,' said the appalling Robert and the order was duly placed.

We will ignore, of our charity, the implied slur on the dietary choices of total strangers. Let us concede that the offending finger, to take only one aspect of this dismal encounter, may have been the cleanest digit on earth, though given the exploratory habits of small boys this is unlikely. It's the suggestion that other people's possessions are of no account and their desecration unworthy of remark that strikes home.

In church one Sunday I placed my copy of the parish bulletin on the ledge in front of me. The seat in front was occupied by a woman, a small boy and one of these enormous shoulder bags capable of holding a suite of furniture. Judging by its angular bulges, this one did.

From the very start Junior made it clear that he didn't think much of the proceedings. He announced that he wanted to go home. Loudly. And frequently.

His mother decided diversion was called for and her eye fell on my copy of the bulletin. She had a sharp, no-nonsense face and she used it to favour me with a glare I was unable to interpret, then or since. Then she seized the bulletin and handed it to Junior.

Within seconds it was in shreds and its entertainment possibilities exhausted. All right, it wasn't great literature. It had no commercial value, unlike the plate of lasagne. Surely, though, the bulging bag could have yielded up some device to keep the youngster amused. But, no, it was up to someone else, to a third party, to them, to provide the means of entertainment. It would have been nice to be asked first, though.

Of course, it happens once in a while that fond parents are brought face to face with their children's shortcomings in circumstances that brooke no denial. I remember one spoiled article of about six who had a vocabulary that would have stripped paint, and he used it freely and on all sorts of occasions. Righteous persons had once or twice complained to his mother, only to be blandly informed that it simply wasn't possible for her darling to know words like that.

Then one day, as little Sean and his devoted mammy were walking along the village street they met the parish priest, who stopped for a chat. Sean had just got a pup and he was leading it home by a string attached to its collar. The pup sat down to scratch its ear. The adults' conversation droned on. Sean decided to put a stop to it, so he grabbed his mother's hand and blunged off. She stood still. The priest jocosely placed his foot on the string. From the soles of his gleaming shoes to the top of his head, the pastor was six feet plus of ecclesiastical dignity but this cut no ice with Sean.

'Take your foot off that . . . string, you big . . .' he said.

Before the word string he had inserted a popular, general purpose expletive of the type his mother said he couldn't possibly know. He might have got away with that. It was when be completed his brisk command with a word suggesting that his parish priest was the offspring of unwed parents that his world changed, changed utterly.

Thus it was that Sean didn't grow up hairy-chested and full of sin. Well, he did grow up and he may be hairy chested, but the last report I heard of him he was remonstrating with some football fans about their language. That's the great thing about public conversions. They may be hard to swallow but they allow no room for back-sliding.

Public repentance doesn't always have the desired effect on young minds. I went to school with a lad whose father was a lighthouse keeper, a fact that may have coloured his views on many things. One day the subject of George Washington and the fable of how he owned up to chopping down a cherry tree came up in class.

The object of that misleading tale was to prove that a full and frank admission of guilt will lead to immediate and generous forgiveness by the injured party. Not so, commented the lad from the lighthouse, there was a legend in his part of the world which proved the contrary.

It dated back to less sophisticated times, when their local parochial house had no indoor plumbing and the toilet was a ramshackle affair perched on the bank of a stream that ran along the bottom of the garden. Unknown hands pushed the rickety structure into the stream one evening, in settlement of some ancient wrong, no doubt.

First thing the next morning the parish priest was in the school seeking the culprit. There are no secrets in the countryside, and there never were, so the pastor's spies assured him that he wouldn't go too far in his search if he began in the school.

He was subtle about it. He told them the story of how the young Washington had supposedly cut down his father's tree, had confessed when challenged and was instantly forgiven. He leaned fairly heavily on the forgiveness angle. In fact he did it so well that the young demolition expert got to his feet and admitted his crime.

He was promptly dragged from his place by the scruff of the neck and the clergyman proceeded to administer summary justice with his walking stick.

'But,' howled the youngster, 'you said George Washington's father forgave him . . .'

The holy man continued to belabour the erring young member of his flock.

'George Washington's father,' he said grimly between wallops, 'wasn't up the tree at the time.'

It's a fact of life that when children want to embarrass their elders in public they do it in style. A yuppie couple, not known to me, invited another couple who are well known to me to dinner at their house. The object of the exercise was twofold, to demonstrate the hosts' accelerating social and material progress and to show off the burgeoning genius of their offspring, a moppet of five years, going on fifty.

The child's mother entertained the visitors with a long list of the prodigy's alleged attainments and the probably imaginary predictions her teacher had made about the glittering prizes that would fall like confetti on her golden head in the near future.

The youngster's father took no part in this recital. He confined himself to scowling over the rim of his Tyrone crystal whiskey glass, which the guests assumed was due to embarrassment over his wife's extravagant claims. They hoped that the somewhat fraught occasion would thaw a little when at last they got to the dinner table. The moppet was invited to say Grace.

She clammed up. No amount of coaxing could persuade her to utter a word. Mummy assured the visitors that she knew it, she really did, Daddy had taught her and she picked it up in no time. In fact she'd said it just before the visitors arrived.

'Come on, now,' she wheedled, 'just say what Daddy said before our guests arrived.'

The moppet's face brightened. Guests and Mummy leaned forward expectantly. Daddy continued to brood over the gathering.

'Daddy said,' the child informed them happily, 'for Chrissake Angela, why did you invite these . . . people over to-night?'

Daddy, in spite of his social, material and educational advantages, and access to the quarter of a million or so words that compose the English tongue, had inserted a popular, cornerboy, present participle into the space above.

All of which goes to show that children really do pick up bad language quicker than their prayers.

Of course they do pick up their prayers eventually, if in amended form. A neighbour overheard her son, newly started school, telling his younger sister to stop doing something or other, because Harold wouldn't like it.

'Who's this Harold?' she asked, suspiciously.

'God,' the little boy replied confidently.

'How do you make that out?' she persisted.

'Och, mammy, you know, Our Far Wart in Heaven, Harold be thy name . . .' was the answer she got.

That, of course, is an exception to the general rule of children dropping you in it in public. Take the case of the women in hysterics on her front doorstep, while her eight-year-old son hopped about from one foot to the other. From the open front bedroom a man's voice could be heard pleading and coaxing. A neighbour or three formed the nucleus of a group of spectators.

'What's up, son?' one of them finally asked.

'Daddy has a bird up in the front bedroom,' Junior nonchalantly replied, 'and Mammy's going crazy about it.'

Instant outrage. The poor woman. The unfortunate child. The insensitive brute. What was the world coming to? People nowadays. Personally I blame television. It's all this running to pubs, and clubs, and all the rest.

Mammy was finally prevailed upon to calm down and tell the whole story to a growing and increasingly sympathetic audience. She had come in from the shops and heard suspicious noises from the front bedroom. She had immediately suspected burglars and, taking her courage in both hands, had thrown open the bedroom door, and found her husband, sure enough, chasing a bird round the room.

As soon as she came on the scene the culprit had taken refuge behind the curtains and refused to come out. She had issued an ultimatum. The creature would have to go. Now. She, for her part, refused to set foot in the house until this was accomplished.

At this point in the narrative there were increasing sounds of struggle from the bedroom, the window opened wider and the cause of all the excitement was hurled bodily out.

She was protesting vigorously at this undignified end to a relationship. Not that anyone could have much of a relationship with a starling, unless, of course another starling. The moral of this story is that you can't put an old head on young shoulders, because the young head full of adult slang can give you enough to think about.

This lad was unusually wordy in his explanation for the commotion. Most juvenile communication is cryptic to say the least, especially when a pair of winsome waifs turn up on the doorstep seeking sponsorship. Small seekers after sponsorship have a peculiar ability to coax into ear-splitting life a doorbell that remains silent under the thumbs of more welcome visitors.

In the unlikely event that the doorbell resists their attentions, the WWs split into a two-pronged attack. One pounds the living-room window with tiny, persistent fists and the other attacks the knocker with totally unnecessary force.

When you open the door you will be presented with a half-eaten ballpoint and a sheet of paper apparently wrestled from a cross dog minutes before. You should, at this point, address the other half of the team.

'What do you do?' you should ask.

'I'm with him,' you'll be told, enigmatically; the only acceptable variation being, 'I'm with her.'

A similar response may be elicited, with patience, from the rest of the retinue, because the pair will have attracted a procession of Pied Piper proportions by the time they get to your house.

The WWs don't know what cause they're soliciting funds for, or if they do know, they're not saying. You will try, of course. 'School' is a fairly predictable one-word response, though 'equipment' or other equally terse justification may be offered for disturbing your repose. Or shower, or bath, or whatever.

You may get nearer the truth on occasion. 'Me bror' is sometimes the motive power behind the WWs. You may wish to pursue this revelation further.

'Where's your brother now?' you may wish to enquire.

'In the house' is the predictable response to your impertinence. You are now face to face with one of the great hazards of the sponsorship minefield. The brother, according to the tattered sheet presented for your inspection, has apparently undertaken to run round the school pitch and for each circuit, attested to by a supervising teacher, you are invited to donate a sum of money.

Since he doesn't have enough get-up-and-go to do the basic

fund-raising legwork, it's unlikely he'll do the more advanced stuff around the pitch. There's not much point in discussing these finer points with his agents. They don't talk in sentences or want to have any truck with people who do.

Children tend to have soundly based commercial instincts. During my teaching days a boy showed me a curious object he had found in a packet of crisps. It proved to be a fragment of frosted, deformed potato and I advised him to send it back to the crisp company with a letter explaining how he had come by it. I saw it as an excellent opportunity to put the English language to practical use. I could see by the look on his face that he preferred not to deplete his meagre stock of the language, nor his energy either, on such a trivial pursuit.

I converted him to my point of view by hinting that the company might send him a packet of the delicacy, free of charge, to compensate him for the trauma he had experienced.

He went away slightly disbelieving and returned shortly afterwards with a reasonably presentable missive, free from the usual range of stains and fingerprints. I taped the inedible piece of spud to it, donated an envelope and a stamp and we sat back to await results.

Three days later he got a letter from the company apologising for the inclusion of the strange object, explaining how their quality control system worked and how they proposed to make it work even better in the future.

All this was over his head, of course, but the postal order for a pound that they had stapled to the letter was well within his comprehension.

If I could have seen the consequences of my actions I would have eaten the offending item myself. Sales of crisps in the neighbourhood around the school reached new heights. Every crisp was minutely inspected before being consumed. Morning and afternoon I was visited by hopeful urchins bearing single crisps on which they affected to see some blemish of life-threatening proportions, although in all cases they consumed the rest of the packet without obvious ill-effect.

All they wanted from me was an envelope, a stamp and the wording of a letter that would bring them back their original investment tenfold. They refused to accept the mathematics involved. The last delegation to which I tried to explain that no company could afford to give away a pound with every few pence worth of goods purchased was led by a suspicious mite who waited until he was safely out of range before yelling at the top of his voice, 'I told yez he wouldn't do it.'

I've often compared the first complainant's good fortune with that of the American senator whose legislative person was bitten by a flea on an overnight train. He complained in writing to the president of the railway and received by return a letter expressing the company's anguish that a man in his position should have been exposed to this indignity.

It was all the more inexplicable, the letter went on, because of the extraordinarily high standards of hygiene for which the company was renowned across the nation. Never before had there been such a complaint, and there would never be another one, because every single measure in existence would be immediately reviewed and improved on, if that were possible.

The company president apologised abjectly and at length, and remained his faithfully. The modified legislator then did what we all do. He looked in the envelope to see if there was anything else, like maybe a cheque, or the typist's phone number or other useful item.

There was something else. It was the president's hastily scribbled memo to his secretary. It read simply, 'Send this guy the bug letter.'

As Dr Johnson said, the usual fortune of complaint is to excite contempt rather than pity. Unless, of course, you're a ten-year-old, for all company bosses were ten at some time or another. And if they've learned nothing else, they should be smart enough to include postal orders – not memos – in their replies to complaints.

17 *The Think Tank*

The Think Tank is presided over by a genial fellow who has spent a good deal of his time on licensed premises and has gained a great reputation for wisdom as a result. He and I constitute the permanent secretariat and the rest of the membership is a variable number ranging from three up to as many as can fit around the table. The avowed object of the group is to advance human knowledge in all directions and at the same time refute the dangerous notion – propagated by reformed sinners, mostly – that only nonsense is talked on licensed premises.

I have known the panel to turn its deepest attention to topics like crime and even offer a prize, vague and unspecified, but somewhere between a bottle of mineral water and a holiday in the sun, for the best example of bare-faced robbery. The competition was triggered off by a panel member with a tale of a friend who came home one day and discovered that someone had stolen his newel post.

I had to ask what that was, and for the benefit of the uninitiated I pass on the definition. It's the post at the end or corner of a stair handrail and there doesn't seem to be much point in stealing one unless, in this age of increased specialisation, some international gang have cornered the market in that line.

There was some debate about whether the next entry should have been allowed, because it had been culled from the pages of a Dublin paper and was not only outside the jurisdiction but wasn't even first or second hand experience. Someone had, in broad daylight and in full view of the staff, stolen a fur-coat from a shop window. And nobody had seen a thing.

An animated discussion followed and one member of the panel went as far as to quote from a television magician who said that when he heard someone describe one of his tricks he couldn't believe it himself.

No decision was arrived at on the matter. It was deferred until a sub-committee could be convened to consider whether the rules could be bent sufficiently to allow it to be included. An entry concerning the theft of a complete set of castle walls in Co. Monaghan, culled from a local newspaper, suffered the same fate. And for the same reasons.

Opinion was divided evenly on the merits of the Labrador and the Apples. In the case of the dog, which had been left tied to a shop grille while the owner went inside, someone had stolen the collar and left the dog. The Apple story was along the same lines. A man with a surplus of apples had filled a barrel and left it at his gate with an invitation to passersby to help themselves. So, somebody had tipped out the apples and helped himself to the barrel.

It was agreed by the panel that both these incidents had a certain merit but they also lacked a certain something, too.

'What we need,' said the chairman, rapping for order with the butt of his glass,' is personal experiences. Have you nothing to contribute to the debate?'

And he pointed his dreaded finger at me.

Well, I offered the Artist's story. This painter is well known in the art world and his work was on display in an exclusive establishment in Belfast where all those who have business have keys and all others must wait until the doorman admits them. The painter came along with his key one day, just in time to oblige a couple of men who were impatiently awaiting the arrival of the doorman. As he told me himself, he was just leaving a few minutes later when he saw the same two approaching the door struggling with several large packages.

Being of an obliging and courteous disposition, he held the doors open while they carried their burdens out. Several days passed before he discovered that he had been actively assisting in the theft of his own paintings.

The panel liked this story, even though I say it myself, but the chairman, a stickler for the rules he was making up as he went along, was less enthusiastic. I hadn't been there, he said, in any capacity at all. It was just hearsay, in his view.

'This isn't hearsay,' said another member. 'I was there when it happened.'

And he launched into the story of the curtains. He and his wife were sitting beside the window of a recently refurbished hotel lounge when she spotted the new curtains. She told him they were exactly the pattern she wanted for their own house. In fact, the way he told it, she paid more attention to the curtains than she did to him. The panel expressed no surprise at this.

She enthused about the curtains to various people in the company at different times during the evening but when they got up to go and she turned to take a last look, all the better to imprint the pattern on her memory, they were gone. The window, like Mother Hubbard's cupboard, was bare. And once again, nobody had noticed anything.

'I don't think I can allow that,' the chairman told him, his voice full of cynical regret. 'You didn't actually see it happen. I'm assuming, of course, that you didn't actually spirit them away yourself to avoid heavy expense later on.'

There was a pause in the proceedings at this point to allow for a ritual exchange of abuse. Only the Shop-keeper's Tale restored the peace. He had gone to a rugby match one Saturday and when he returned to his car the boot was open and the spare wheel was gone.

'Big deal,' said he of the Curtains story, in disgruntled tones, 'in Dublin and in this town, too, it's the whole car that's usually stolen.'

'My jacket was taken, too,' said the shopkeeper.

'In this town,' the Curtains man went on,' they deal in whole suits. There are places where you just put in your order, wait a few minutes and before you know it, your man's back with your new outfit . . .'

'But,' the retailer continued patiently,' I had five hundred quid, in a clear plastic bag, shop takings, laying on top of the spare wheel. They left that behind. Of course some of it was in pound coins. They're a bit of a giveaway in those parts.'

'As daylight robbers,' the chairman ruled, "they weren't up to much.'

'The pound coin,' an associate member of the Think Tank put in, 'is something you rarely hear a good word about. Even thieves don't seem to want them, if that story's true. However, an aunt of mine has discovered a new and interesting use for them. She stacks them up in the little divisions in her ice-cube tray, covers them with water and keeps them in the fridge.'

'Now that,' said a full member, 'is as fine an example of raving lunacy as I've ever heard of. I hope I don't regret this, but why does she do it?'

'She's an impulse buyer,' the associate member replied. 'This is a kind of aversion therapy. She converts all cash not vital for day to day needs into pound coins and freezes them. They become frozen assets, if you like. Then, if the spending bug hits her she knows the notion will be off her by the time she's thawed them out.'

'Let's all go round to her house and see if she'll hand out any scotch on the rocks,' the full member suggested.

'No chance,' the associate member told him. 'She has embraced teetotalism as part of the new thrift drive. There'll be no fiver's worth of ice in a drop of the craythur up in her house.'

'That's a good story,' the chairman interrupted coldly, 'but the subject is theft, not thrift. I'll have to instruct the secretary to delete it from the record.'

'All right,' retorted the associate member, 'You're so smart. You tell us one. All you've done so far is criticise our efforts. Come on, speak up or shut up.'

The chairman rose to the challenge, and narrated the Tale of the Doberman and the Hambone. The chairman has had a varied and colourful career, which included, at one stage in his youth, a spell with a firm that laid underground cables for the Post Office. Among his colleagues was a fellow large on brawn but short on both brain and conversation, not to mention the finer points of etiquette. His eating habits were, well, unusual, so when he produced a hambone one day as part of his lunch, nobody took much notice.

A Doberman did, though. The men were working in a prosperous suburb and the dog lived in the house they were working outside at the time.

The dog was well-heeled. He lived in considerable style in suburban detachery, with a chauffeur-driven car at his disposal, an infinite variety of gate-posts and lamp-posts for his personal convenience and the fat of the land to live on. But he wasn't satisfied with all this. He seized the hambone.

The workman wasn't the type of fellow to let his bone go with the dog. He hurled himself on the Doberman and there ensued an epic struggle between the two primitives that not only astounded the chairman and his workmates, but which was passed into folklore in that part of Belfast.

The dog eventually conceded defeat and relinquished his loot. The workman – and the chairman was emphatic on this point – resumed his own savaging of the hambone without giving it so much as a wipe. Adversity hadn't made him a finer person in any way. The entire panel paid a hearty, laughing tribute to this narrative, but the associate member wasn't satisfied.

'I'm not sure about that one,' he said. 'I seem to remember that Mark Twain once observed that if you pick up a starving dog and make him prosperous, he won't bite you. He said that was the principal difference between a dog and a man.'

'It's a nice theory,' I put in, for I had been quiet for a long time, an unusual thing for me. 'A well-to-do dog should, on the surface of things, be better disposed to humanity than one on, or just below, the breadline.'

'Mark Twain said something else,' the chairman added. 'He said some days it just don't pay to get up. None of you appear to have noticed that while this profound debate was raging, the shutters have been pulled down. All in all, the standard of entry for this competition has been very poor. The meeting's adjourned.'

Of course Herself thinks I go out every Thursday night to enjoy myself. . .

18 *Donovan's Nephew*

Time was when anybody who was anybody went on the Big Sunday excursion from our town to Portstewart. The Promenade was patrolled by herringbone-suited gentlemen, with raincoats slung casually over their shoulders, indulgently overseeing the lower orders seeing the holiday season to an end on the last Sunday in September. By the time I was earning folding money, however, anybody could go on the excursion, the splendour had departed entirely and the organisers had trouble filling their bus.

Someone managed to cajole Donovan into going one year and, not being one to suffer alone, he informed me that I was invited too. He presented me with a ticket at his expense and let me know that if his generosity troubled my conscience I could always balance matters out by attending to such trifling matters as lunch, tea and any liquid refreshments we might get, strictly unofficially in the latter case.

That Sunday morning was fine, with the promise of a good day, and, as I sprawled on the seat outside McNamee's pub waiting for the bus to arrive, I began to feel quite cheerful about the prospects and possibilities of a day at The Port. Then Donovan arrived and cast a gloom over the proceedings.

'What's wrong with you?' I asked.

'We have to take the nephew,' he growled and slumped on the seat, the picture of misery.

Visions of a day spent minding a spotty child rose before me and in imagination I had fished the brat half a dozen times out of the harbour before I thought to enquire how old he was.

'He's fourteen and a bit,' said Donovan glumly.

'Well, that's all right then,' I said, vastly relieved.

'It's not all right,' snapped Donovan. 'You don't know this lad. He's a bad article.'

'He can't be all that bad at fourteen and a half,' I thought aloud.

'Listen,' said Donovan. 'Last summer, during the mission, he left the chapel early one evening and stole Master McBride's car. He knows as much about driving as I do about making pastry and he hit the bride a wallop that nearly pulled the wing off the motor.'

'Well, what happened?' I asked. 'Was he hurt?'

'Hurt,' snorted Donovan. 'Hurt nothing. It's a good job, though, that old McBride is a decent man. He settled for getting the dents fixed. My sister said the young rip would have to pay for it all himself, and do you know what he did? He got a couple of books of cloakroom tickets and sold them all round the place at a bob apiece. The prize was a goose.'

'The punters much have been peeved when they found out there was no raffle and no goose,' I said.

'There was a raffle all right,' said Donovan in heavy tones, 'And there was a goose. The wee twister stole that from Master McBride's yard as well.'

I devoted some thought to the possible twists and turns the future of this enterprising young man might take.

'Why have you to take him with you today?' I asked, just to show I was taking an intelligent interest in the conversation.

'My sister,' said Donovan, in the tones of one explaining two and two to an idiot child, 'is a great cook and I can cook none at all. This is the price she's charging me for a few Sunday dinners.'

'Cheer up,' I said with fake enthusiasm, 'We'll get him paired off with some nice wee lassie and let her mind him.'

'The Lord Almighty,' said Donovan with totally uncharacteristic piety,' couldn't mind him, not even if he was bolted to the floor.'

At this point the subject under discussion arrived. He looked, as all rising young villains invariably do, like the archetypal choirboy, except that he appeared to have no finger-nails on hands that were covered with nicotine back and front.

Donovan wasted no time on conversational niceties. He introduced me, then he held up a hand the size of a ham, uncurled a finger about the size of a banana and poked his young relative in the chest.

'Listen to me,' he said. 'You behave yourself this day or I'll fix you.'

The nephew was unimpressed. He winked at me, rolled his eyes heavenwards and stepped on the bus. As we passed underneath the town clock a presentable wee girl in a blue coat turned round and smiled in our direction.

'We'll be all right,' I told Donovan, 'She'll take him off our hands.'

'God look to your wit,' said Donovan, still in pious vein.

As we disembarked at Portstewart the nephew made his sole effort at conversation.

'That's a lot of water,' he remarked innocently.

'That's only the top of it,' growled his uncle. 'Any of your nonsense and you'll see the bottom of it.'

The day passed uneventfully enough. Little Miss Blue Coat latched on to the nephew and Donovan and I wandered about in our predatory way, alternatively chatting up the girls and exchanging amiable abuse with our numerous acquaintances from all over South Derry. It was after teatime that I noticed the shoulder that Blue Coat's head was resting on had changed shape. I nipped across the street and studied the situation from close quarters. The nephew had gone.

Donovan invoked the aid of a large number of deities, some heathen, some not.

'If there's a card game in this town,' he told me grimly, 'that whelp's in it.'

'There's a card game somewhere up that entry,' said Joe McKenna, who was strolling past at that moment. 'I'm nearly sure I saw Jack Rainey heading up there.'

'I hope you didn't,' said Donovan and we sped across the street to the entry. It was guarded by a tough-looking citizen, who by standing in the middle of the opening and leaning the palm of his hand against the wall effectively denied us admission.

'Where do you think you're going?' he demanded, without moving. 'I'm looking for my nephew,' Donovan told him in a voice that shook windows along the street.

'I'm not deaf,' growled the tough-looking custodian.

Donovan had graduated with honours from the street-corner school of repartee.

'Y'are so,' he mouthed silently.

The custodian took his hand off the wall and cupped it around his ear.

'Eh?' he asked.

It was enough. Donovan was through the opening in a flash and the guardian, assuming us to be bona-fide card-players, let us go.

We could hear voices coming from a store halfway up the entry. We cautiously peered through a pane of glass in the top of the door. The nephew was sitting at a table consisting of a door laid across a couple of boxes and facing him were three decidedly unsavoury-looking characters. The scene was lit by a naked bulb on a looped piece of flex. I could see by the working of Donovan's ears that he was in the grip of a powerful emotion.

'What's happening?' I asked.

'See that joker facing us?' whispered Donovan. 'That's Rainey. I wouldn't cheat him and hope to walk again this side of Christmas. I don't know who the other two are but any company Rainey's to in is bad company.'

'What's the nephew doing?' I asked.

'You're not going to believe this,' said Donovan. 'He's cleaning them out. With the three card trick. You've never seen the like of it.'

If he had said the Indian rope trick it would have meant just as much to me.

'You'd better put a stop to it,' I said, without exactly knowing how or even why.

'Is your head away?' demanded Donovan. 'I wouldn't make myself known to those three boys for anything. If I did I'd never be able to go out again after dark.'

At that moment Rainey stood up and my heart stopped.

'We'll go,' he growled. 'We'll go while we still have the price of a drink.'

We flattened ourselves against the wall but the door opened outwards and mercifully hid us as they strode down the entry. The nephew was shutting the door when Donovan spun him round and in silent fury relieved him of twenty-three pounds and some small change. Twenty-three pounds disappeared into Donovan's pockets, the rest he handed back.

'Take that,' he said. 'Get yourself an ice-cream and a bag of sweets. You known where the bus is. Get up there and sit in it. Every time I pass that bus I want to see your head at the window. When we get home, and if you get home, I'll give you back this money. But I'm warning you, give me one more scare and you'll see neither home nor money.'

There were limits beyond which no one, not even a villainous nephew, would go with Donovan. The conqueror of Rainey and company quietly closed the mouth he had opened in protest and slunk away. We followed at leisure down the now unguarded entry.

'Thank the Lord that's over,' said Donovan fervently.

'Amen to that,' I added.

'Don't mention it,' said the Lord. 'I know you two of old. We'll be doing business again.'

I didn't mention this to Donovan. You know what he's like.

19 *Con Tricks*

The pavement was wide and busy but I knew as soon as I saw him that we were on a collision course. I moved to my left as he bore down on me, the tails of his Crombie flying behind him, and in the way these things happen he veered to the right. I changed course and he did the same, so we ended up facing each other.

'Stand there and I'll walk round you,' I said, and he smiled indulgently at the quip I've always wanted to use but never got the chance to deliver until that moment. As I drew level with his right shoulder, treating him like a roundabout, he laid a restraining hand on my arm.

'It is you, isn't it?' he said, peering closely at me.

I've been me as long as I can remember and a bit before that, but I had no idea who he was. That's one of my constant problems. No memory for faces.

'Still up in . . .?' he asked, twitching his head in a comprehensive sweep that took in the entire city and most of the province. I agreed that I was still up in wherever he had in mind.

'Still the same old team, I suppose?' he went on, releasing my arm and eyeing me with the pleasant smile of a man who has unexpectedly encountered an old friend.

I agreed that the old firm was still intact, whatever it was, for my mind was busy elsewhere, trying to identify this prosperous fellow who was not too busy or important to stop and talk to me.

'The lads must be big now,' he continued and I assured him that they were bigger than I was and gainfully employed. He said it was marvellous the way time flew.

I felt it was time I did more to keep my end up in this conversation, so I asked him how he had been getting on.

'Powerful,' he said, 'Never felt fitter, fit as a flea, look at that,' and he did a kind of a dance step that sent shoppers scurrying out of his way.

'Mind you,' he said, suddenly confidential, 'I couldn't have done that a month ago. In fact, two months ago I was sure I'd never walk again.'

The situation was getting out of hand. This man, whom I clearly ought to know and who knew all about me, had been through a bad time and all I could do was stand there wondering who he was. His eyes narrowed slightly.

'You did know about the accident?' he asked, and there was a tiny, well-bred note of hurt, even disappointment, in his tone.

There was nothing for it but the truth. I admitted my guilt. I knew nothing of his accident.

'Oh, it was a simple enough thing,' he told me, 'I just stepped off the pavement and this joker came round the corner on the wrong side and that was it. Fourteen weeks in the Royal, hooked up to all kinds of pulleys and things.'

'I'm very sorry to hear that,' I told him, and I meant it. 'I'd have been in to see you if I'd only known.'

'Ah, don't worry about it,' he said, with a wave of his hand. 'I'll be all right. There'll be compensation, of course, and I might as well tell you, I need it. Welfare State, big deal. Not one single penny did I get of any kind of benefits since the day and hour it happened.'

He took hold of my arm again.

'Lend me a tenner,' he said.

I looked at him again and noticed that the Crombie had been slept in. The shirt I had taken for white was actually greyish, the club tie had been in contact with many unidentifiable substances, the shoes were cracked and no razor had visited his chin for a day or three. He knew his business, though. By visiting guilt on me he had diverted my attention.

I didn't give him a tenner, or even a fiver, but I liked the way he told his story, so I made a small donation that I'm sure did the broken veins on his nose no good at all.

I saw him once more and that, by coincidence, was the very next day in a city centre pub at lunch-time. He was facing a mesmerised young couple having a snack.

'Welfare State, big deal,' he was telling them. 'Not one single penny did I get of any kind of benefits since the day and hour it happened.'

I caught the young man's eye and shook my head in warning, but the girl was already opening her purse. There's one born every minute, I thought, but then, who am I to talk. At least I met him only once, which is more that I can say for the Bangor Gardener. I thought for a while he had adopted me.

'I'm just up from Bangor,' he would say. 'I'm looking for a wee job at the gardening but there's nothing going,' and he would wave his arms resignedly at the glass and concrete of the city centre, puzzled beyond words at the dearth of gardens to be worked in.

'Would you help me to get back to Bangor?' he would ask me, and I always did, though I used to wonder aloud to him about the wisdom of going back there, since it's a town well supplied with gardens. Still, he preferred to do his gardening in Donegall Place, where the work was lighter and probably more profitable.

I find that persons looking for ten pence for a can of beer are irresistibly drawn to me and, since I'm as fond of a bargain as anyone else, my stock line is, 'Here's twenty pence, get me one as well.'

The first time I used this line, the suppliant said no, he only needed ten pence to make up the price, thank you very much, sir, you're a decent man.

It's the only time the line every worked. The more usual response consists of two words. One is Off and the other, though of four letters, isn't 'Push.'

I'm not even safe from these predators on my home turf. A vision clutching two plastic bags materialised in my garage one Saturday afternoon. One minute I was sweeping the garage floor – statistically I get more punctures in my own garage than anywhere else, so I perform this task with meticulous, if unavailing, care – the next I was being accosted by a female person. Her voice had preceded her.

'Would you like to buy something for charity?' was the disembodied opening shot. I looked around but there was only me. When you start to hear voices, you're on the threshold of a mystical experience, I thought, but mid-day on a Saturday seems to be an unusual time. Then the owner of the voice, complete with carrier bags, stepped from behind my car and demolished my barely formed image of my garage as a place of pilgrimage for future generations. She repeated her request.

'Buy a nice purse for the lady,' she ordered me briskly, fishing one of the hideous articles from the depths of a carrier bag. I couldn't see myself presenting it to Herself under any circumstances, not unless I observed the ancient superstition and put folding money in it. I didn't want to give her ideas after all these years so I ruled out the purse.

'What about a nail-brush?' my visitor demanded, delving into the other bag. I declined the nail-brush. Also the sponge.

'What charity do you represent?' I asked her.

This was mere stalling. She wasn't leaving without a contribution because I could see she was one determined lady but I wasn't prepared for her answer.

'Me,' she said in ringing tones, 'I'm very poor.'

Now that sort of devastating candour deserves some sort of reward, however modest, though I declined her tentative offer of goods in exchange. She was following a trend that began with tinkers and clothes pegs, who were in turn replaced by the man with the little brown suitcase.

No matter when he called, he had always been discharged from the chest hospital the previous Thursday. In proof of this assertion he wheezed at length, before, during and after his sales pitch. His case contained half a dozen folding coathangers and a few other odds and ends. According to his story a charitable group had set him up in business, 'just to give me an interest, like, sir.'

In all the years he told me his story the rust stains on the folding hangers remained in mute proof of low stock turnover. They continued to bring in the revenue, though, and that must be every entrepreneur's dream. Buy once, sell forever.

Some operators don't bother with either goods or a hardluck tale, preferring the straightforward 'Gimme' approach. This species, with an apparently suicidal streak, seizes his victim in the middle of the road. The victim, preoccupied with crossing in a single piece, is instantly demoralised – I speak with authority here – by the vice grip of the pointed fingers that almost meet through sleeve, flesh and bone and the mournful expression, on the verge of tears, on the tapper's face.

'Good luck to you, sir, and God bless you,' said one of these operators to me in Dublin when I bought my freedom from him, 'I'll get the wife and the childher to pray for you.'

'Why don't you pray for me yourself?' I asked, moving my arm to get the circulation up and running again.

'Because, sir,' he answered loftily, 'Prayin' is woman's work and childher's work.'

And off he went, the only real demarcationist I've ever met in my whole life.

20 *Panting for Liberty*

You should never wear your best trousers when you go out to fight for freedom and truth. The thought is not mine. It's the property of Henrik Ibsen who became famous by writing plays about dolls' houses and similar codology.

Seduced by the fame brought about by his dramatic activities he gave up philosophising about trousers and so a great source of wisdom was lost to the world. If he had stuck to his true vocation we might have had some sound advice on the subject of socks, shoes, shirts, ties and jackets, and perhaps in the fullness of his maturity, a few profound observations on overcoats.

It seems a pity to stop short at trousers and limit the restrictions to freedom and truth. A blanket prohibition on wearing your best trousers, assuming you possess more than one pair, should get serious consideration.

Ownership of trousers, plural, was once a symbol of wealth on this island. There was a man in a MacGriana short story who was described as rich because he owned three pairs of trousers. Of course, trousers come out as singular in the ancient tongue. This idiom used to give rise to much merriment among less fervent Gaels and led to unseemly speculation about whether the well-heeled fellow had actually been a Manxman with the obligatory three legs. He was nothing of the sort. He was just a run of the mill Donegal man and he rates a mention in literature because he lent a pair of his trousers to a lad who was getting married. Whether this was a neighbourly thing to do, and whether freedom and truth suffered in the inevitable, subsequent marital struggle, is something Ibsen, and the rest of us, might have given some thought to.

Of course, he may not have lent his best trousers. Donegal men know, as we all do, that things that are lent often come back damaged, accompanied by unfulfilled promises to foot the repair bill. And sometimes things lent don't come back at all.

You should not wear your best trousers, for example, when you go down to your local garage to buy petrol, check the battery and the tyres, and, most important of all, check the oil. I know what I'm talking about here.

You see, it's while you're doing this last operation that a jovial acquaintance happens along and passes the time of day.

Now if he would just stand there with his hands in his pockets and talk about the weather or the finer points of foreign policy, like a normal person, the best trousers wouldn't come to grief. He doesn't do that. He steps up quietly behind you and smacks you cordially between the shoulder blades.

You instantly assume you're being mugged. You utter words that would get you expelled from the Meths Drinkers' Annual Convention. You bang your head on the bonnet. And worse, much worse than all this, you drop the dipstick.

It falls, wrong end up – a feat in itself – on the top of the air filter. The vibration showers your best trousers with drops of oil, just the way a wet dog splatters you with water. The evidence of the dog's gesture will disappear. The mark of the dipstick, like the poor, will always be with you.

You don't realise this at the time. The 'What about ye, oul' son,' that accompanies the wallop between the shoulder-blades, not only dispels the dread of mugging but distracts your attention as well. In fact you don't even notice the damage until you get home. I certainly didn't until I walked into the kitchen and found Herself perched on a stool drinking coffee and reading the morning paper. She didn't look up but she said 'How did you get oil on your trousers?' I wish I knew how she does that.

The mugging sensation returned, reducing the throbbing from the crack on the head to a distant murmur. More expressions, suitably excited, were uttered. The merry crinkle of folding money going up in smoke joined the medley of sounds. A resolution to throttle the jovial idiot, although emotionally satisfying, had no effect on the stains. A neighbourly slap on the back, like the touch of the master's hand, had transformed the brand new into the second best.

'Ah, sure it was an accident,' said a voice on the edge of consciousness, and maybe. All the same I wish I'd paid more attention to Ibsen when I had the chance.

Trousers lead almost inevitably to socks and more philosophising, because deep thinkers down the ages have devoted a remarkable amount of thinking time to matters of apparel. You take Immanuel Kant (b. 1724), for an example. He was an expert on such heavyweight stuff as the theory of knowledge, ethics, logic, metaphysics, maths, physics and aesthetics. But, of course, you knew all that already.

The good doctor wrote books explaining his views on all these subjects and I'm assured by people who know about such things that his views carry a great deal of clout to this very day.

In spite of all this erudition, Immanuel Kant (d. 1804) couldn't cope with his socks. This is no idle jest. He had the greatest difficulty keeping his socks up and a lot of the time he devoted to the problem had to be diverted from the ethics and logic business.

Part of the problem was that in his day trousers ended at the knee. This fashion recurs every few years and is hailed by each generation as the latest thing, as far as women are concerned anyway. From the male viewpoint it matters not a scrap whether a fellow's socks are up, down, or non-existent, the trouser leg hides all. Poor old Kant lived in more demanding times when people were inclined to notice your socks.

They were no problem to the average citizen. He just tied a piece of tape round the top, called it a garter and went on about his business. Professor Kant recoiled in horror from such a device. He feared, indeed he was totally convinced, that it would play havoc with his circulation. Which just goes to prove what old Will Rodgers said, there's nobody as daft as an educated man once you get him off the thing he was educated in.

Kant, however, wasn't prepared to go about with his socks hanging down, since that would have been a bigger hazard to his health, his neck in particular. Knee-length trousers meant knee-length socks, after all. So he invented the suspender belt. This is not something his fans prefer to remember, being more inclined to drool over his Critique on Poor Reason (1781). His invention has, of course, been hijacked by the same people who subsequently made knee-length trousers their own.

Any fellow wearing Kant's device these days will rapidly become the subject of letters to the world's agony aunts. And that's only the beginning of his woes.

Old Immanuel's device was spring operated, came in pairs and was housed in special trouser pockets with tapes running down to each side of each sock. It's a pity, a real pity, that a man so imaginative couldn't have progressed logically to the Greatest Sock Question of all: what do washing machines do with odd socks?

A brain used to grappling with the laws of the universe could surely have envisaged a machine that would eat socks. If he could devise a gadget to suspend them from, complete with cogs and springs, he must surely have known that he had sown the seeds of conflict between material and machine.

Man simply has never been at ease with his socks, a fact which washing machines grasp instinctively and exploit ruthlessly. First there was the problem of the toes wearing out, then the heels, and by the time human ingenuity had eradicated these weak spots by inventing a material indestructible by anything except fire, the washing machine entered the fray. Put X socks in the washing machine and $X - 1$ will emerge.

All life forms, animal or vegetable, adapt to their surroundings in the interests of survival and the principle was modified in the eternally triangular struggle between Man, Machine and Sock. Just as the polar bear blended into the Arctic landscape and the tiger into the jungle, sock patterns changed to prolong active life.

The gaudy designs of yesteryear that compelled attention without threatening self-respect gave way to sombre colours. All this was necessary to reduce the washing machine's capacity to reduce the sock stock by fifty per cent at every washing. Plain socks in packets of two or three pairs meant that the worst could never happen. There would always be two matching socks.

That was the theory but the inscrutable, evolutionary process seems to be coming full cycle. Packets of two or three pairs are still available but in two or three colours. The machine quietly swallows a sock at each washing, leaving the other alone in a two-footed world. Not just alone, but useless as well. The answer may be in Kant's Critique of Practical Reason (1788) but I can't afford it. My book buying budget is being eaten into by socks.

It may well be that the sock-eating washing machine is peculiar to the Kelly household, a manifestation of some ancient malediction originating at the dawn of time or thereabouts. It occurs to me to mention this when I recall the Mystery of the Missing Shoe.

I bought a pair of shoes one time and wore them only once. That was when I tried them on in the shop and found them good. It occurred to me about a year later to give them an outing and when I opened the box there was only one.

There followed a searching and a ransacking the like of which has never been experienced before or since. Everybody who could be blamed for the disappearance was duly charged but eventually acquitted for lack of evidence. After a while I got fed up looking at the single shoe and threw it in the bin. There's a remarkable shortage of one-legged men seeking a right shoe in my size.

Two years later the missing shoe came home. It remained tight-lipped, as they say in newspaper circles. I've never found out where it had been, what it had been up to or whether it had made its fortune. All I know is that it had been living in a plastic bag. If I had observed that ancient precept about keeping a thing for seven years, I would have had a brand new pair of shoes miraculously restored to me. The celebrations marking the return of the prodigal son would have been nothing compared to the whooping-up I'd have indulged in for having these lost soles return home.

Sometime between discarding the first one and the return of the second one my youngest, embroiled in homework one night, asked me for an example of irony. For the life of me I couldn't think of one. I could now but now, of course, she knows all the answers. She's still young enough to know everything.

Especially about ties. There's something about ties that defies logical analysis. Women have strong, if incomprehensible, views on the subject. A friend of mine got two, that's right, two ties from his wife for his birthday. He appeared at breakfast the following morning wearing one of them.

'What's wrong with the other one?' she demanded suspiciously.

There is no possible answer to that question. The problem with ties is that they make statements, sometimes about you, occasionally about whoever bought it for you.

The statements may be lies, of course. There are people going about wearing ties that proclaim them to be graduates of a college whose name they couldn't even spell. It's not unknown for men who wouldn't know the different between a football, a tennis ball and a snowball to be decorated with ties that identify them as members of football or tennis clubs. This gives rise to some interesting misunderstandings.

'I know all the sporting ties there are,' a fellow said to me once, 'but I can't identify that one you're wearing. What sport is it anyway?'

I could have lied to him, because know-alls have that effect on me, but I didn't, because whatever sport I mentioned was bound to be one he knew. In any case the tie had nothing to do with sport. It was just a tie, designed, as all ties were meant, to hide shirt buttons or the lack of them, or to catch the drips from coffee cups or other forms of liquid refreshment. I told him that and he didn't believe me anyway.

My youngest remarked severely on ties that display evidence of recent food intake. The tie, she was certain, had a function other than to catch stray fragments of soft-boiled egg. Or sauce. She was particularly inflexible on the subject of sauce.

This led her on to the subject of shirts, a topic close to my heart. Not that I have strong views on shirts as such, more the number of pins concealed in the brand-new variety.

Now this is something I have researched thoroughly and I can state with authority that a new shirt may contain up to thirteen pins. If you're superstitious that number may strike you as somehow significant. It certainly was for me. I found only twelve during my first reconnaissance. The thirteenth stabbed me in the ear when I pulled my shirt over my head.

Experiences such as this have led me to develop a more methodical approach to new shirts. These days I lay the new purchase on the bed, still lurking in its cellophane wrapper, and I go away for a while. Then I sneak back to see if it has moved or anything. I try to creep up from behind, or from one side. This cautious approach once led to the capture of five pins and two plastic dofors resembling miniature bicycle clips.

Of course I suspected that there ought to be more pins but an inch-by-inch search failed to reveal any, so I put the shirt on. Number Six then stabbed me in the throat.

My youngest wasn't concerned with these niceties. She was

exercised more by the plunging necklines of blue string vests under shirts that once were white. They lacked a certain something, as far as she was concerned, and bits of what appeared to be hearthrug spilling from openings in the superstructure were even less impressive. This is a viewpoint widely shared.

A macho type came into our local watering hole on a night when the temperatures were of the level that led to the cremation of Sam McGee, and his shirt was open to the waist or thereabouts. He wore the standard quota of chunky jewellery, including neck chain and ornament.

'Aw Gawd,' said one young woman, 'it's Medallion Man.'

'Naw,' said her friend, with her eyes on his chest, 'that's Donkey Man.'

Don't draw any hasty conclusions from all this. After all, if Medallion- or Donkey Man had been wearing a tie, he'd never have been noticed in the first place.

21 *Mouse-hunting*

A uncle of mine, a man of profound wisdom, once advised me that anyone who meets a mouse, should it be in Africa, to quote his exact words, should kill it at once because if it's not on its way to do harm it's on its way back.

I've always tried to follow this advice conscientiously but I'm no Nimrod. I haven't encountered all that many mice and those that have actually crossed my path generally demonstrated amazing turns of speed and manoeuvrability. And a reluctance to lay down their lives. I can understand that. I don't like it but I can understand it.

I did develop some skills in mousehunting after a weekend of torrential rain and gales brought down the chimney of Kelly Towers. There is a connection between all these events which might not be readily obvious but all will become clear eventually. A bricklayer came in response to my summons and told me that before he could contemplate scrambling about on my roof I should first purchase and have ready two bales of hay.

I thought he was joking but he wasn't. The idea was to sling one on either side of the roof tiles to form the basis of a platform for working from.

I duly presented myself at the market and asked for two bales of hay. Nothing could be simpler, I thought. I was wrong again. Hay is usually bought and sold by the load, so that anyone who turns up looking for a paltry two bales, and without a faint smell of horse clinging to his person, isn't exactly a big-spending customer. The salesman asked me what I wanted it for and I told him.

'Hay's too dear for that,' he told me generously. 'Straw's good enough.'

Two bales of straw were dragged from the back of the pile and loaded into the boot. I stored them in a corner of the yard. When the bricklayer arrived he decided he could do without them so they stood in the corner of the yard covered with polythene until I got fed up looking at them and dumped them.

Not long after the repairs were completed, Herself reported that a mouse had strolled in March hare madness across the kitchen floor. A foolish mouse, for she's not the type to spring on a chair and holler for help, being much more likely to pursue it with blunt instruments and abuse.

An interesting few days followed. We took it in turns to loiter in the kitchen with intent to cause injury. The intruder maintained a low profile. Well, he would. They're a low-slung species anyway.

It's amazing the number of experts on the subject of mice you can meet. I'm excluding cats. We didn't have one then, but I would have thought the mere presence of the howling multitude that squat on the back garden wall from time to time would have had some psychological effect on the mouse. The only thing that had any effect was a sharp smack from a coal shovel. This only worked because the first expert we consulted had prescribed a sticky substance to be laid in the miscreant's path. They were creatures of habit, he assured us, always following the same track.

The corpse was unceremoniously dumped and peace descended. For one whole day. It was at the end of that day that I formulated the view that all mice look alike. The next one was the image of the recently deceased. Unlike his twin, though, he had no taste for a sticky end. I consulted another expert. He poked a hole in a sheet of paper with a pencil.

'A mouse could get through a hole that size,' he told me. 'Seal off all entrances and exits.'

There followed an outbreak of house-repairing the like of which was never seen before. Every cupboard was moved, every skirting-board was inspected and sealed, every loose floorboard was screwed down. The place became draught-proof. I was in places where the hand of a man had never set foot since the house was built. The mouse continued his serene trespassing.

It wasn't all a total write-off. In the meter cupboard, which would have been a tight squeeze for a pygmy, and which nevertheless I sealed tighter than a drum, I found two razor-sharp chisels. There from the building, no doubt, but all mine now.

Then a neighbour said she'd had the same problem and found that the trespassers had taken up residence in her carpet sweeper. It was a long shot, but the morning after I got this news I inspected a redundant carpet sweeper that lives in the back of the cloakroom.

It was mouseless, but I still had it in my hand as I stepped into the kitchen and discovered the lodger had finally let familiarity breed contempt. He was stuck in the middle of the sticky stuff.

I folded over the cardboard the goo was spread on, bashed the mouse-sandwich once with the carpet-sweeper for every time I'd cracked my head on the meter-cupboard door-frame and cast the bundle into the exterior darkness of the bin.

That, happily, was the end of the invasion, though not of the mystery of how we had been chosen for the honour. That was cleared up a couple of months later when I happened to fall into conversation with a man from Balmoral market and he told me how popular the haystore was with mice. Straw-bales were more frequently occupied than hay-bales, he added, because there was a much quicker turnover of hay.

'You brought your mice home in the straw,' he told me.

And the stuff was never even used. Still, two days of sealing up the house had a bonus, apart from the bumps, grazes and strained ligaments, though we didn't discover that for another couple of months. That was when the plumber came to replace the back-boiler and found the desiccated remains of two more of the invaders. The sealing operation had driven them back into the space behind the heater and below the boiler.

They had come to the hot and final destination I had so fervently wished for them.

22 *Exercise is Bunk*

I was savouring a small refreshment and minding my own business when this man that I knew slightly, and didn't know anything good about, slapped a glossy leaflet down in front of me.

'What about one of these?' he demanded. 'It's just what you need.'

It was a picture of a very presentable young lady. A bit smug looking, I thought, but then she had much to be smug about. Or not a lot, depending on how you like it distributed.

'It's a very civil gesture,' I told him, 'but I foresee several difficulties. Herself may be hard to win round. She has strong views on this sort of thing.'

'Not the girl,' he said, a bit testily. 'The bike, man, the bike.'

'A bike,' I pointed out, 'has, among other identifying marks, two wheels, hence the name. This yoke has none at all.'

'You're just trying to be awkward,' he said. 'It's not for going places, this bike. It's for getting rid of the avoirdupois. Observe its finer points. The cushioned seats. This control increases the resistance of the pedals. And look at this little clock. It tells you how far you've travelled.'

'But you haven't travelled anywhere,' I told him. 'The thing's on a stand.'

'This is in your imagination,' he replied tersely. 'You just fix some destination in your mind and off you go on your imaginary journey, slimming as you go, shedding the flab.'

'I resent these references to flab,' I remarked. 'I can't deny it but I resent it. Anyway, all I can see is the leaflet. Have you got one of these machines?'

'It's in my other suit,' he answered, sarcastically. 'In fact, I only have the one, slightly used model. I'll tell you no lie, I need the money. I had a bit of a misfortune with a horse yesterday and the wife's birthday is tomorrow. It's a bit of a laugh, really. She bought it for my last birthday.'

'It'll be your last birthday, all right, if she finds out you're trying to sell it. Whoever buys it just might find it being repossessed,' I advised.

'You're not interested, then?' he said, preparing to move on down the bar.

'Sorry,' I replied. 'But you know, it reminds me a bit of that

O. Henry story, where she sells her hair to buy him a watch-chain, and he sells the watch to buy her a set of combs and . . .'

'I saw the movie,' he snapped and departed in search of a less resistant buyer.

I had a certain amount of sympathy for that man. Exercise bikes, like other outward manifestations of the slimming hysteria sweeping the nation, tend to be bought by third parties as presents, broad hints or downright threats. And they do tend to have a novelty value which wears off rapidly. Many a garage, or spare room, up and down the land has an exercise bike, or a rowing machine, maybe a set of weights, even an exercise mat. Closer inspection will reveal that many still have the price tags, or bits of the original wrapping, still attached. And remarkably little sign of wear.

Everybody wants to be slim but the devil has the best tunes. A colleague of mine plays a furious two hour game of badminton several times a week, pausing only to take quick sips of a diet soft drink. Then she and her fellow-players go off and eat chip sandwiches. A chip sandwich, with scalding hot chips and fresh bread, is one of the devil's tastier inventions. Which is why, I suspect, that one of the badminton players is several pounds heavier than when the keep-fit mania started.

Some people are completely impervious to this form of insanity. One night Herself and I went to a restaurant which I shall not name in case people think we can afford to eat there. She eyed the menu with some alarm.

'At these prices there should be a cabaret,' she observed.

And there was. It was unofficial and provided by half a ton of Ballymena men who arrived shortly after us and took a table for four in the middle of the room.

You could see right away that they enjoyed their food. The leader of the quartet draped himself – I choose the word with some care – on his chair and dominated the conversation. In every restaurant I've ever been in there has always been one person whose voice and views are unavoidable. This was another such diner.

He decided what each would eat and why, and from the moment he arrived and until the four of them left, he entertained us all with a comprehensive and scurrilous review of his friends, relations, in-laws and out-laws. No preacher ever got the undivided attention that was paid to him.

You could tell by the backs of the other diners' heads that nobody wanted to miss a word. All around the room shoulders shook with suppressed laughter as he discoursed on his brother-in-law, one Harold.

Harold had phoned him on Sunday morning to see if he was going to church, but indeed he was not, for he had to take a shower and cut his toe-nails; but he did none of these things, for the very instant the disappointed Harold rang off, our man was off like a shot to a pub in Carnlough. And do you know who was there?

He then named the entire clientele, and this, mark you, was in the days before Sunday opening, too. He gave us all a complete rundown on the social and professional status of each of the illicit drinkers and catalogued them as decent men or rascals as appropriate.

This monologue was punctuated with 'D'you want that wee bit of steak?' and 'I'll just take that wee bit of fish if you're finished,' to the other three, each of them busy pretending he wasn't with them. But he was and he'd eaten most of their dinners and their Black Forest gateaux as well as his own, and, as they went, the very floorboards creaked their approval.

'Don't you ever turn out like that,' Herself said to me, and it wasn't the talking she was referring to, but the belt-buckles that pointed at the ground. And the word diet began to creep ominously into her conversation over the next few weeks.

Personally I think that one day somebody will prove to the satisfaction of a lot of people that all the things that are currently bad for us are actually beneficial. At present everything you enjoy is either illegal, sinful or fattening. In some cases all three.

Now you just take breakfast, which, as A. P. Herbert once remarked, is the critical time in matrimony. He didn't mention cholesterol, but maybe it hadn't been invented then. In spite of his omission, he had a point. Breakfast is the time when you're most likely to have your conscience examined by a third party. I have reason to believe, though I cannot really prove it, that more questions are asked in the house at that time than any other. I abandoned the ritual a long time ago, having profited from the experience of numerous acquaintances.

One of them went into a downtown eatery for breakfast and asked for a cup of tea and the sole, remaining, visible slice of toast.

'It's stale,' said the woman at the counter. 'I'll make you some fresh.'

'It'll do me rightly,' said the customer.

'I'll only be a minute . . .' she began.

'Wait till I tell you, daughter,' the customer informed her earnestly, 'I'll take it. If I wanted an argument over breakfast I'd have stayed at home.'

It was a modest enough way to start the day, a slice of toast and a cup of tea. There are others, dedicated weight-watchers some of them too, who, if shown a breakfast menu offering a full English, Irish or Scottish breakfast, depending on the country, will have it, on the grounds that cholesterol and calories consumed away from home do not enter either the bloodstream or the waistline. And there are some, of course, who take their domestic habits with them.

'Bring me two eggs fried rock-hard,' said a man I know to a waitress in an English hotel at breakfast-time, 'burn me a couple of slices of toast, and it must be black on both sides, mind you. Oh, and a pot of shamrock tea.'

'What's shamrock tea?' asked the bemused waitress.

'You throw three tea-leaves in the pot and top it up with lukewarm water,' he told her.

She brought him his strange order and asked, one assumes with well-disguised sarcasm, if there would be anything else.

'Yes,' he told her, 'there is. Sit down there. Ask me what time do I think it was when I got in last night. Give off about the state I was in. Ask me why I'm wearing this terrible tie. Nag me. I'm homesick.'

I would take a small bet that that man never heard of A. P. Herbert and his breakfast theory but there you have two minds with but a single thought anyway.

If there are some who take their breakfast-time ethos with them wherever they go, there are others who take their breakfasts instead. I will never forget the crystal-clear image of a man running for the bus of a morning with a fried egg dangling between the finger and thumb of his right hand. His briefcase was trapped tightly under his left armpit and his left hand was stretched out, palm upwards, with the correct fare positioned on. And, like stalactites, slices of fried bacon hung from between his fingers.

We shall never look upon his like again. This is not a eulogy for his passing because he is still alive, though whether he is well is something I cannot speculate on. The continentals, leaner, fitter and bossier, with coffee-and-a-roll breakfasts, are making his breed extinct. Even so, I'm mindful of the fact that when a perfectly preserved mammoth was excavated from 40 feet of Siberian ice a few years ago, its mouth was stuffed with food. The food, like the mammoth, was also perfectly preserved, but the consumer was dead, let there be no mistake about that.

Our whole attitude to food, fat and slimming is hilariously ambivalent in this country. You just look around on any of the dark days between December the 25th and January the 1st and then you'll see the Ghost of Christmas Past jog by. He'll be wearing a brand-new tracksuit and a pair of running shoes that would give you palpitations if you knew the price of them.

He'll likely be wearing a species of luminous Sam Browne belt as well, and what you're looking at is irony on two legs. Her Indoors has decreed that he should first of all stuff himself with every conceivable form of fattening substance over the holidays, then work it all off in the athletic gear she thoughtfully bought a month or two before.

There's an element of premeditation in all this that's chilling in the extreme. If the feasting doesn't polish him off, then the carbon monoxide or the casual savagery that passes for driving in these parts may bring in the bonuses of his insurance policies. There's no point in telling this man that the inventor of the craze he's following popped his clogs – well, all right, running shoes, then – while out jogging. He'll find out the truth soon enough, one way or another.

I was eating a bite of pub grub in a place renowned for its cuisine one time and I was talking to the proprietor about this and that when a woman came in and took him aside. They talked in low tones for a while, then she pressed a small, brown-paper parcel into his hands and departed.

'Do you know what that is?' he asked me.

'It's a small, brown paper parcel,' I answered, because I'm as sharp as a tack in some matters.

'It's a canned meat pie,' he told me, and named the brand. He then went on to explain that the woman had charged him with the sacred responsibility of delivering it to her son, then living in Switzerland. The publican was leaving for a holiday in the same expensive country that very evening, which is a point, by the way, that you might care to reflect on.

'She takes a motherly interest in his nourishment,' I commented.

'Wait till I tell you,' he said. 'He's a chef in the best hotel in Geneva.'

So there you have another culinary viewpoint. Good old home cooking prepared with a tin-opener was clearly superior to anything a high-flying chef might dish up for his well-heeled patrons. And that's not as far removed from filling the other man up with turkey and sending him out to play among the traffic as you might think.

You can understand now why I have a sneaking regard for the man who claims that there are two forms of pure food left, one being fish and the other whiskey. I'm inclined to subscribe as well to his reservation about fish, expressed since they've begun to glow in the dark.

Now don't misunderstand me. I'm as game as the next man to have a go at the dieting, and the exercising, not that I have a lot of choice since Herself was in the audience on the Night of the Ballymena Men. I have to add, though, that once or twice I've experienced odd side-effects.

There was the day, for example, I was walking through a city centre shopping precinct, when the sun was shining, God was in His heaven and all was right with the world. Except that breakfast, such as it was, was hours behind me and lunch, equally unexciting, wasn't due till the end of the century. Still, I was prepared to put up with all that, for Herself had assured me that if I would only stick at it I wouldn't know myself. How right she nearly was.

Ahead of me two girls in well-filled red skirts and white blouses were pushing a trolley laden with sandwiches and every male head in the vicinity, mine included, was turned in their direction. Except that everyone else was looking at the girls and I was looking at the sandwiches. As I realised the implications of this – and wondered if this was what Herself had in mind – a long forgotten incident from my childhood floated up from the subconscious.

A neighbouring farmer had called to buy some seed corn from my father, and the pair of them leaned against the tractor in the yard while the prospective buyer examined a handful of the product. As they talked the rooster began to chase a hen round and round the tractor.

The neighbour, satisfied with the seed, threw it absent-mindedly into the path of the amorous pair. The hen raced on but the rooster stopped to eat.

'Dan,' said the neighbour to my father, 'I hope I never get that hungry.'

They both laughed and I didn't know why then, but I did that sunny morning in the shopping precinct, many years later. That traumatic experience forced me to rethink the whole dieting and exercise question. The trick is to think thin and eat what you like, and, of course, wear a size bigger in everything. That takes care of the dieting.

As for the exercising, remember the immortal words of Henry Ford. 'Exercise is bunk,' he said. 'if you're healthy you don't need it and if you're sick you shouldn't take it.'

Of course he wanted to sell us cars.

23 *Profane Matters*

The French have a saying, things are against us. In French, of course, the idea comes across in a more Twilight Zone sort of way. What it comes down to, simply, is . . . inanimate objects seem to have a mind of their own. You know how it is. Just take your eyes off the last screw for that bit of self-assembly furniture for one minute and it's gone. There is, naturally, a foolproof way of finding it. Take off your shoes and walk around the area where you think it might be. You'll find it. The god who presides over these matters is telling you something.

One Saturday I finally ran out of excuses for not making an extra cupboard we've needed for a long time. It's of the kind of awkward dimensions that can't be bought, so with the cunning of the born procrastinator I got all the parts cut to size in the do-it-yourself shop. All I really needed, apart from enthusiasm, was my faithful electric drill and a fine bit the same diameter as the screws.

I possessed two of these bits at one time but I broke one and never got round to replacing it. However, all I needed was one anyway.

Every so often I had to swop it with the countersink bit and that's when disaster struck. I put the fine one down in a safe place at one point and when I came back for it, it had vanished. I reacted by the use of a carefully selected stock of expressions that I keep for moments like this. The job was only half done. The shops were shut. The work was at a standstill.

Then out of the blue, a frequently expressed belief of a long-deceased aunt surfaced in my mind. When she lost or mislaid anything, she immediately called on the patron saint of lost things. And Saint Anthony, she used to assure me, invariably delivered the goods. I thought I might as well give the idea a whirl.

'Anthony,' I said, for I believe in informality in these matters, 'you see how things are. If the bit doesn't turn up, the job just won't be finished. The world and his wife are getting ready to go out, for it's the weekend, and just between ourselves I think it's a lousy deal if I can neither get this cupboard finished nor get a piece of the action, as our American cousins say.'

The silence from on high was deafening. I assumed that the saint had heard my earlier comments and decided to restrict his aid to those purer of heart and vocabulary. So I rummaged halfheartedly in my biscuit tin of assorted odds and ends for a reasonable substitute. And I found the missing bit.

I hadn't put it there. I'd put it on the bench at the other end of the garage but I didn't stop to unravel the mystery. I simply noted that I owed the aforementioned Anthony a suitable gesture of gratitude and got on with finishing the job.

When I was tidying the garage floor I found another bit. I had only one to begin with. Now I had two.

I think I could rationalise that development . . . eventually . . . but when I came to tidying the bench I found the one I'd put there in the first place. So then there were three, smug and identical, leaving me with much to think about.

So much so that the completed cupboard stood empty for a long time. Considering the miracles of multiplication associated with its construction it seemed less than respectful to put anything into it at all. As I reflected on what would be chosen to put into it and what was to be cast into exterior darkness, for some reason, the saga of Annie and Joe rose unbidden from my subconscious.

In the long ago, as the old-time seanachies would have put it, when the world was a lot younger and its occupants a lot less sophisticated, Annie and Joe lived in our town.

Annie was massive and it is almost a cliche to add that her husband was small. They lived in the town's Top Row and they considerably lowered the tone of that dental-sounding location, for Annie was a virago by nature and Joe was a labourer by profession.

He was as affable as she was aggressive. He performed his labouring duties in a crumpled grey-striped suit, a collarless khaki shirt and an Andy Capp-type cap, his concave face split in a permanently amiable grin. Local legend had it that the grin was permanent because Annie, in a rare moment of affection, had playfully tweaked his cheek and left him deformed for life.

Annie, in turban and wraparound overall, with brawny arms folded under a massive bosom and a cigarette jammed firmly in the corner of her mouth, spent her daylight hours at war with humanity from her front doorstep.

Those who had pretensions to grandeur in the Top Row found the presence of the ill-assorted pair a sore tribulation. Not that they heard much from Joe for he would only answer Annie back from a safe distance and even then he generally allowed himself only one devastating comment before fleeing for his life. His utterances were carefully collected by the local connoisseurs and passed around like the rare gems they usually were. One is worthy of mention, if only for its unerring accuracy in fixing Annie in the mind's eye.

Joe was slinking off to the pub one Saturday afternoon instead of doing whatever Annie had decreed he should about the house, so she was leaning out of the window hurling abuse after him. He wandered on until he was almost out of range, then he turned.

'Get your head in out of that, woman,' he roared. 'You're making the house look like a horse-box.'

Joe and Annie were the opposite of that calm that's supposed to exist in the centre of a cyclone. They were the permanent storm in the erratic calm created by everyone giving them as wide a berth as possible.

Although Annie could agree with nobody about anything and Joe could rarely see eye to eye with Annie, there was one subject on which there was a measure of unanimity between them and that was Martin, their sole offspring.

He had inherited neither his father's puny frame nor his mother's enormous proportions. He was tall, slim and broad-shouldered and by the time he was twenty he had won every worthwhile prize at every sports meeting in County Derry. Many a marriageable maiden viewed him with a speculative gleam in her eye.

Annie took a simple, uncomplicated view. There was no girl born, or ever likely to be, good enough for her Martin. Joe was a bit more flexible. A well-doing girl, and he conceded that such a creature might exist, could aspire to Martin, especially if, as the local phrase had it, there was a roughness of money in the family.

Then Anne Mahoney came from England to live with her aunt and uncle in the Top Row. She was as pretty as summer and she fell for Martin right away. Before the month was out she was spending all her free time from the local hospital gazing adoringly up at Martin as they wandered hand in hand about the countryside. It was some time before Annie discovered the awful truth, but when she did, her rage was terrible to behold.

She immediately laid siege to the Mahoney household, standing under a tree opposite their front door and howling abuse like a demented banshee with a smoker's cough. The Mahoneys gave up the use of their front door and slunk in and out by the back.

This obvious stratagem somehow escaped Annie. When she could see no Mahoneys about she transferred her thunderous attentions to their other relatives dotted around the village. Anne and Martin furtively continued their romance.

Such was the grip of terror that Annie's tongue imposed on the community that there was no reaction at all, none, that is, until it all came to the Canon's attention. He was surveying his domain from the steps of the parochial house one summer evening as Joe trundled past on his way from work.

'Joe,' he called, crooking an imperious finger, 'Joe, come here a minute, I want to talk to you.'

Joe, with grin firmly in place, approached the presence.

'It'll have to stop, you know,' said the Canon, without preamble. 'You must assert yourself as head of your household and put a stop to your wife's scandalous behaviour.'

Joe squinted up at his parish priest.

'Ah, just how would you do that, Canon?' he asked, adding, somewhat unnecessarily, 'She's a fierce big woman.'

In south Derry, fierce can mean very, as well as what it says. Joe meant it both ways. It didn't escape the Canon's notice that Joe had said 'you' and not 'I.' It was well known locally that Annie had little time for the cloth at the best of times, but if she thought the Church might take the Mahoney side in the marriage question there was likely to be a confrontation of historic proportions. The Canon considered all the implications.

'Well, what do you think of the match, Joe?' he asked eventually. Joe's grin slipped slightly.

'I'm for it,' he said seriously. 'I'm all for it and that's the truth.'

There was no money in the Mahoney connection but he saw the commercial viability of a nursing qualification.

'Well, then,' said the Canon grandly, 'go home and tell her so.'

Joe's grin vanished and his mouth fell open in fright.

'She'd kill me,' he told the Canon with simple conviction.

The Canon had not reached his exalted position for nothing. It was, in any case, an innocent age when uncomplicated solutions were adequate.

'Not if you sprinkle her first with holy water,' he said with the touching simplicity of absolute faith.

Joe looked up at the setting sun and down at his boots, his amiable grin swinging back and forth like a skipping rope as he appeared to consider this novel, if impractical solution. He said nothing but went on his way, shaking his head at the wonder of it all.

That night the Annie-watchers reported only one brief outburst, followed by an inhuman scream, just about tea-time. There was silence for the rest of the night and speculation was rife. One school of thought held that Joe had finally mutinied and paid the supreme price. Next morning, however, Joe emerged, intact and grinning, and ambled off to work, so speculation shifted to the notion that Annie was in a coma induced by some incredible act of defiance on Joe's part.

Curiosity reached fever pitch by the end of the week, for Annie was neither seen nor heard for the next three days. The following Monday evening, amid continuing silence from the Top Row, Annie and Martin appeared at the parochial house to make preliminary preparations for their wedding. The Canon, secure in faith, kept his own curiosity under noble restraint and got on with the formalities.

On the day of the wedding he leaned over and spoke to Joe as he stood expansively beside the strangely subdued Annie outside the church.

'The holy water worked then, Joe,' he said confidently.

'Well, now, not at first, Canon,' said Joe, grinning hugely. 'But it worked grand when I boiled it.'

24 *Junk Mail*

I've been deeply concerned for some time about the declining quality of junk mail. My personal experience goes back longer than I want anybody to know about and I feel that I can state with some confidence that the stuff thudding through the letter-box these days isn't a patch on the offerings of yesteryear.

The first unsolicited item I ever received was a pork pie. Viewed from a purely aesthetic standpoint it was a thing of beauty, six inches in diameter and four inches deep. The pastry was golden brown and the floral shapes that decorated its top had been crafted with consummate artistry.

It was packed in a sturdy custom-made box. The address was neatly typed. The postmark was Melton Mowbray. It may well be that there is, or used to be, an establishment in Melton Mowbray renowned for its pies. It may also be the case that the same company thought that casting its anonymous pie upon the waters would bring back business a hundredfold. And anonymous it was. Whatever lay behind this unexpected gift must remain forever one of the great mysteries of our times, up there with the more profound questions, like where flies go in the winter time.

There was no accompanying leaflet, no name, no hint of either origin or donor, apart from the postmark. The item was delivered to my lonely shieling in my student days and would have fed most of the residents in that warren of bedsitters. It would have, except that nobody wanted any of it.

Well, naturally, I felt obliged to explain, in so far as it was possible how I had come by it and this raised some doubts in the minds of potential consumers. One ingrate even went so far as to quote from some heathen source about the practice of Oriental potentates having special tasters, guys whose job it was to sample the royal grub before the boss tried any of it. The logic, it seems, was that if some malcontent had poisoned the dinner the slave would give adequate warning by dropping dead on the spot. No reason was given as to why I was chosen for a similar honour, but the splendid pie was consigned to the bin without so much as a toothmark anywhere on it.

A contemporary fared even better, because he had the good fortune to share his surname with a famous drink and when the distillers were celebrating some anniversary or other they sent him a bottle of their product. He consumed it without ill-effect, other than the hangover traditionally associated with this form of indulgence. Of course the brew had arrived in a sealed, labelled bottle and was accompanied by a letter explaining the reasoning behind the ploy.

It also revealed that the bottle was meant for somebody else, a person of consequence and influence, but he didn't draw attention to this instance of mistaken identity. Somewhere, I feel sure, a disappointed public relations officer wondered for a long time why his brilliant idea hadn't resulted in massive free publicity for his company's wares. And something of the same disappointment may have been experienced by the sender of the pie.

I've never got anything since to compare with that pie but the flow of junk mail continued unabated. I've been offered once-in-a-lifetime pictorial plates, never-to-be-repeated double-glazing offers and five European languages for a song. I could have laser-effect thingummies playing on the ceiling for a few pounds more and I've been offered bargain sets of matching luggage which put the unworthy notion in my head that, having failed with the pie all those years ago, someone will settle for my leaving the country.

As for cameras and calculators, car phones and trouser presses, hair-driers and revolutionary gadgets for home heating, the offers stretch in never-ending line like Wordsworth's daffodils. The snag with this deluge of correspondence is that all the senders want money. The pieman didn't. Once in a lifetime there is such a thing as a free lunch. And I blew it.

Some of these appeals come from afar. I treasure one from Kuala Lumpur, although in fact its contents originate from Boulder City, Nevada. This is not to be confused with Boulder, Colorado, but of course you would never commit such a geographical gaffe. I don't know why this item should have been mailed from Kuala Lumpur, which is nowhere near Boulder City NA or Boulder CO. I don't even know why it was sent to me or how the sender came by my correct postal code, something a few of my friends never mastered, in spite of the best efforts of the Post Office and myself.

The first item out of the envelope, well, plastic bag, actually, was a copy of a newspaper article whose modest headline proclaimed it to be The Most Important/Money/Power/Romantic-Love Discovery Since the Industrial Revolution. Sub-editors the world over have been cut down in their prime and left wandering the streets, broken men, for writing shorter headlines than that.

The four-page tabloid job was an interview with a one-time professional card-player, author of a best-selling poker manual – his words – and prolific inventor. And he had invented something he wanted to share with me. It was a mysterious process called Neo-Tech which would enable me to prosper anywhere on earth and under almost any economic or political conditions. That's what the man said.

The process also applied to all money and power-gathering techniques, to all situations involving the transfer of money, power and, would you believe, love.

The first thing called for, though, was the transfer of cash to Boulder City, NA. The second item in the clear plastic bag was a remarkably versatile order form, which accepted a round dozen currencies and all major credit cards, including the aptly-named Carte Blanche.

The inventor admitted that he stumbled on his amazing but undefined discovery while playing cards and he was very helpful in listing the characteristic of the traditional cheat. Anyone proposing to fiddle in a big way had only to eliminate the give-away signs and they were in business. He confessed that that was not his main intention, because his unspecified recipe for success was ethical and honest. And if I'd got a move on and ordered the package within seven days I'd have got the inside information on stock prices, job-power – whether that is – and controlling others.

This moving appeal brought the immortal words of that other great twentieth century folk hero, J. R. Ewing, to the forefront of my mind. Ole JR said his role in life was to take money from the poor and give it to the rich. It's a sentiment not limited either to the oil industry or soap opera.

There are times, of course, when the arrival of a junk mail item can arouse suspicion in the most laid back mind, even mine. Among my treasures is one which reminded me at once of the little man who worked for the same company for years and years. Day in and day out he sat at his desk and moved papers from the in tray to the out tray, unwrapped his ham sandwiches at one on the dot, left on the stroke of five and came back next morning to start the whole thing all over again.

Year after year young whippersnappers joined the company. They moved up. They moved sideways. They moved out to and on to greater things. They wore good suits, they drove cars and they certainly didn't spend the lunch-hour at their desks munching ham sandwiches.

The wee man observed all this and wondered at it. And, as he wondered, a new and exhilarating emotion stirred beneath his sensible woolly vest. One day he startled everybody by rising from his desk in mid-morning, a thing he had never done before, and storming into the manager's office in such a fury that the manager retreated into a corner by the window where he fenced himself in by pulling out all the drawers of the filing cabinets.

In a voice that vibrated every window in the building the wee man demanded a raise. The manager, sensing that he was in no immediate danger, emerged from his fortress of filing cabinets and asked him why.

The wee man told him. At the top of his lungs.

It boiled down to this. Everybody about the place was getting a lot more money than he was. Even the doorman. He wasn't going to put up with it any longer, so he wasn't.

The manager produced a file and showed him that far from still being on the tenner a week before deductions he had started on thirty years before he had received an annual increase just like everyone else. Indeed, the manager remarked, they used to wonder what he did with all his money. For example, why didn't he drive a wee car or even go out to lunch once in a while.

The wee man read the file, then he sat down a while, deep in thought.

'I'm sorry about all the rumpus,' he said at last. 'You see, my wife never told me about the raises.'

All right, I wouldn't have believed it myself but then one day a letter arrived and I discovered that I was the managing director of a great enterprise. Some are born great, some have greatness thrust upon them, but I achieved it painlessly and unbeknownst to myself. I was the M.D. of O. Kelly Ltd. The chest swelled with pride.

I didn't know what the company did. The firm of protective clothing manufacturers who wrote to me seemed better informed. They reckoned I was in the market for something called tractor suits. Obviously I must have tractor drivers somewhere in the far-flung reaches of my enterprise, though I certainly wouldn't have employed the lad who modelled the tractor suit. He stood a lot closer to the razor than any tractor driver I ever saw, his finger nails were clean and the shock absorber he was carrying over his right shoulder sparkled a bit too much for my liking.

He was sharing his page with a hardy-looking character modelling a dynamite jacket – that's what it said – and an amiable-looking fellow wearing a donkey jacket. There was a time in my life when the donkey jacket was the badge of office of either a foreman or a charge-hand – and none of them were all that amiable, as far as I can recall anyway.

Whatever my company produces it's a noisy, sweaty business. There was a clue, perhaps, in the square-jawed surveyor or surveyor's mate on a neighbouring page. He has a theodolite over his shoulder and he is staring in the general direction of another rugged specimen in a waterproof gale suit, whatever that's for. And why, I wondered, was the man next to him wearing flame-resistant overalls.

I don't know what the food's like in my canteens but the staff look terrific. My waitresses wear Kelly green – naturally – and because I'm apparently indulgent to all employees, they qualify for outdoor coats. They wear these, I imagine, when they ferry the snacks out to the surveyors and the hard men in the flame resistant overalls.

It was all puzzling. Here I was, a power in the land, an economic force, but I didn't seem to have the same standard of living as the heads of other big organisations, like Ford or ICI. And then, as through a mist, I seemed to recall another bulky envelope arriving, addressed to my social secretary. It disappeared so swiftly I thought for a long time I might have imagined it.

I wonder if Herself is keeping something from me?

25 *Don't Wish You Were Here*

When people recommend things to you, run. They're out to get you for some reason or another. It's up to you to figure out what.

My own enlightenment on this subject arose from a guesthouse recommendation. For many a year we had holidayed happily in the town of Dungloe, as indeed we continued to do for some years after this episode. This particular year we were sidetracked by a completely unsolicited testimonial to the wonders of another guesthouse in a different part of Donegal. The lady doing the recommending was, as the peculiar Irish expression puts it, no goat's toe and she backed up her effusive tributes with a dog-eared brochure fished up from the depths of her sizeable handbag.

Since we're very democratic in our house, at least until the bills come in, the verdict was in favour of giving it a try.

The ancient Romans, before embarking on any sizeable enterprise, had the gruesome habit of killing a sacred chicken or two and studying their entrails for signs of success or otherwise. If I had been able to lay hands on a chicken and submit it to the same indignity, I fancy I would have found the omens unfavourable. My first communication with the place drew a reply on a yellowing jotter page of ancient design, with fragments of wood still embedded in the paper. It began with the unforgettable phrase, 'An answer to your letter . . .'

It would be unreasonable to expect culinary expertise and grammatical accuracy from the same hand, I thought, as I tried to silence the small, still voice that cautioned 'Beware.' I sent off the deposit as requested and in due course we followed it.

The same chicken, if we had employed one, might not have indicated that the roofrack would blow off on the M1, to the consternation of numerous other drivers and the detriment of our personal possessions. I doubt if its accuracy would have pinpointed the total obliteration of a tyre near Dungannon, since all mechanical contrivances came along after the philosophy that called for its disembowelment in the interests of prophecy.

I'm sure, however, that it would have indicated something ominous about our arrival at the guesthouse. Nobody had ever heard of us. Nobody had ever written to us, though the cheque for the deposit had been cashed with commendable speed. No rooms were ready and we were advised with remarkable candour that there was nothing for the dinner either.

Our informant had assured us that the place had won some species of award, but if it did it was in the last century, if not the one before. The hallway was floored with what appeared to be narrow, parallel trampolines concealed under ragged carpet. As you passed each item of furniture, it leaned confidentially towards you, so that you half expected it to say, 'Did you hear the one about . . .?'

The bedroom doors opened as you approached, although no unseen hand or electronic wizardry was at work; it was simply a matter of ancient locks that had long since given up the ghost. I discovered that it was possible to keep the door shut by replacing the inner knob with a safety pin. I made this discovery by accident when the knob fell off and rolled away irretrievably under the wardrobe.

There's probably some explanation for a safety pin being able to do what the heavier knob couldn't but I had no time to devote to research. It was the safety pin which had previously operated the wardrobe door. It lounged against the wall several feet from the wardrobe, which had no means of hanging or storage whatever. The window, painted shut, hadn't moved in a generation.

As we contemplated this remarkably poor return on our investment, a voice from outside the bedroom door demanded to know what we would like for dinner, adding significantly that we could have sausages.

This subtle hint was augmented with the intelligence that the butchers would soon be closing, but whether for the day or from lack of business wasn't clear. We had sausages, just for the hell of it.

After dinner we set out to find the beach. According to our informant, it was two hundred yards away. Your man in the seven league boots might have considered it a couple of hundred yards. As it was we never found it. We did, after an hour, find a kind of disused quarry which, presumably, was what was meant.

We fought our way back up the briar-tangled lane from the quarry to the highly recommended guesthouse. The brochure, I could clearly recall, mentioned nightly entertainment.

The entertainment turned out to be a fiddler called Packy who wouldn't be coming because he was busy with the turf, on account of the weather having improved unexpectedly. The only other amusement, and I use the word with some feeling, was provided by the bar's other two occupants, a pair of decidedly intoxicated locals who knew only one word between them. It was a simple four-letter job that they applied to every man, woman, child, object and area of endeavour. One of them kept making drinking motions with his mouth and gullet but emptying the beer down the front of his shirt and all over the bar. There was no cover charge.

In the morning we gathered our belongings, sacrificed our deposit and fled to Dungloe. When I got back home I decided, after a few days' reflection, to stage manage a meeting with the owner of the dog-eared brochure who had spoken so fulsomely of the guesthouse. There was a For Sale sign on her house with Sold plastered across it and I found out that she had gone to England. I never discovered what I had done to deserve her malicious attentions.

Of course it doesn't always follow that because a bed and breakfast establishment looks presentable that it is in fact so. Once when we were on our travels down the west coast of Ireland we booked into a very upmarket class of establishment, unknowing that a family feud simmered and bubbled in the background.

The man of the house seemed ill-suited to the role of host. He thundered through the house, wrenching doors almost off their hinges and slamming them behind him with completely unnecessary violence. He combined all this frantic activity with ignoring us in a pointedly aggressive manner. He would vary the routine by hurtling out of the house, leaping into his car and screeching away in a stench of burning rubber. He would return within minutes in the same rally-driving fashion.

On his trips in and out of the house he carried briefcases, maps and bundles of papers, which made me believe not only that he was some kind of bureaucrat but also that democracy was in some danger at his hands.

I got the impression that he wasn't too keen on his wife's involvement in the hospitality business. She appeared to behave as if none of this was happening but there was a dangerous calm about her all the same.

I felt quite sympathetic for her having to put up with this troglodyte behaviour but my compassion was both tested and proved ill-founded the next morning when everything looked set for the kind of breakfast that has now been exposed as bad for us.

It was when I lifted the teapot that I sensed a definite change in the atmosphere. She was poised by the door like a sprinter on the starting blocks and she sprang into action the instant the last dribble of tea left the spout.

'The wood,' she yodelled, 'the wood,' and bore down on me like a coastguard cutter. I didn't know what I had done but I clutched the teapot in semi-defensive posture and hoped that Herself would bring up reinforcements in the event of all-out attack.

In my decadent youth the cry 'To the woods' had been made popular in a student magazine and enjoyed a brief vogue as a facetious invitation to receptive young women to frolic in the forest. At first hearing the landlady's cry seemed like a west coast variation but it did seem a bit brass-necked, especially as Herself was seated opposite. I can also remember thinking, in the time it took the landlady to bound across the room; that I might one day fall on hard times and be glad of any diversion I could get, but as far as I was concerned the time was not yet ripe.

'The table,' she said, as she drew up alongside, 'the table.' She indicated the teapot stand and I finally got the message. There she stood poised, I thought apprehensively, to do me a mischief of serious proportions and so I placed the teapot, with exaggerated care, on the dofor provided for the purpose. I couldn't begin to imagine what horrendous experience had made her assume that I would do otherwise, but I did my best to reassure her.

'I know it's a table,' I told her. 'We have one at home.'

Clearly she didn't believe me.

It was a judgement on me, I suppose, for not going to Dungloe that year either, and the gods rammed home their point when we reached Carraroe and it was snowing. It's not supposed to snow in August, even in Carraroe, but I lent the Polaroid snap of the white stuff on the ground to a man in Donegal the next day and I never got it back. You'll have to take my word for it.

I should have made Donegal in daylight that day except that some wiseacre had been fooling with the signposts at Maam Cross and I travelled in circles for a while. It rained all the way across Sligo and my passengers sprawled in various undignified postures, sound asleep, secure in their misplaced faith that I would get them all to where we wanted to go.

Beyond a faint suspicion that I was finally somewhere in Donegal. The roads were deserted. Any visible lights were up the sides of mountains with no apparent means of access. The people of Donegal were sticking close to their firesides that miserable night.

I came round a corner and there, practically on the roadside, was a cottage with light spilling across the roadway and a car standing at the door. I pulled in behind it, went over to the door and raised my hand to knock. As my knuckles descended towards the door it opened and I almost punched a splendidly bearded Capuchin monk on the nose.

This is not going to be one of those stories. He was real, I think. We looked at each other for a moment and I recovered sufficiently to say I was looking for the way to Dungloe.

'I'm going there myself this very minute,' said the holy man, 'Just follow me.'

He got into the parked car and off he went, like a bat out of that place monks and other clerics are supposed to be dedicated to keeping the rest of us out of. Before I got my car door shut his taillights were twin specks in the distance. By the time I had got into second gear he had disappeared so completely that I began to think I had imagined him after all.

I got to Dungloe without any help from him and the sun was shining the next morning, when we set out for Aranmore regatta. I don't suppose any of us had much idea what a regatta consisted of. We expected boat races, bunting, colour, bands, excitement. We got the rain again.

In fact we ran into the Carraroe weather recycled just at Burtonport. The boatman spread a polythene sheet over us and I got the bit with the hole in it. By the time we scrambled off the boat at the Aranmore pier I was wet through and there was no room left under the only tree on the island.

I took the only practical step I could think of to ward off pneumonia. I took my socks off, wrung them out and stuffed them in my back pocket. then I went to watch the athletic events. These were races of varying lengths and for varying age groups but they all had one thing in common. They were all won by the same competitor, a hulking youth with more hair on him than a donkey and wearing a T-shirt advertising a well-known beer. He won the under-18, under-16 and under-14 events but the one that called suspension of disbelief was the under-12. He may have won more but like all the rest of the spectators I had left to watch a brawl between two rival gangs. It turned out they were on the island engaged in that timeless pursuit of the fior-Gael, learning Irish.

A brawny islander waded in and administered rough justice impartially to both sides and I elbowed my way into a nearby pub where, as is traditional in Donegal pubs, there was room for one more. I found myself seated beside a man I was sure I knew. He was an associate professor of Humanities from an American university and I didn't know him from Adam. He had consumed a good few shots of firewater and was being disrespectful about those giants of Irish literature, Joyce and Yeats.

The same pair had caused me some grief as a student, so I warmed to the man and we took a small refreshment together. He spoke with some affection of Patrick Kavanagh and ended by singing 'Raglan Road.' All present joined in. They didn't know a word of it, of course, but they groaned more or less tunefully and the party was in full swing when a messenger arrived with two items of news. The ferry was back and the sun still shone on the mainland.

We trooped down to the pier in the rain and were duly accommodated under the polythene once more. And again I got the bit where the hole was. When we disembarked at Burtonport the pier was baking in the heat and numbers of tanned and lobster-coloured persons were swaggering about. You could tell they were jeering at us inwardly. I gave the professor a lift back to his hotel.

'One for the road,' he commanded, so I drove into the hotel carpark and we took up our positions in the bar. Suddenly the professor leaned over confidentially.

'Can I ask you a question?' he said. 'A personal question.'

He then held up a hand and assured me that I didn't have to answer, that I had the right to remain silent, or something to that effect.

'Go ahead,' I replied expansively.

'This is my first time in Ireland,' he told me, 'so I'm not right up to date on your Irish customs and traditions. So tell me, why the hell are you wearing your socks in your back pocket.'

The mention of socks brought a vision of the Capuchin of the night before into my mind, so I told him the story. He listened intently.

'What's all this got to do with your socks?' he asked when I was finished.

'Well,' I explained, 'Capuchins don't wear socks and when you asked me about my socks it sort of brought the episode back to mind.'

'I'm going for a swim,' he said. 'You Irish just kill me, you know that, you just kill me.'

As I walked down the car park the Capuchin swished past and got into his car. I didn't see him come and I nearly didn't see him go. He departed in a screaming of tyres, leaving a smell of burning rubber behind him, the way his arch enemy is supposed to leave a smell of sulphur.

I would like to have told him about getting to Dungloe without his help the night before. I would like to have commented on his driving. It also seemed relevant to tell him about the professor's puzzlement about my socks. But he was gone.

I set off down Mill Road into the town. It was a gorgeous afternoon, the kind that makes you think it will never rain again. A motorist going the other way blew his horn and waved at me. I glanced in my rear view mirror to see who he was and realised that both my rearview mirror and my car were still in the hotel carpark. I turned wearily back to collect it.

When you've been wet and dried twice in the same day without a change of clothes and you're walking along a sunlit road in a holiday spot, it's truly astonishing the number of well-dressed, clean acquaintances you meet. You can see the puzzlement, or the disapproval, or both, forming in their minds.

I thought of explaining the whole scruffy situation to one or two of them but in the end I didn't bother.

Holidays can be so confusing.

26 *Getting the Fingers Burnt*

It all started off simply enough, as disasters always do.

'Would you like to buy a ballot ticket?' this clean-cut young man asked me.

Now I'm not used to ballot sellers who talk in complete sentences. When they turn up on my doorstep they usually order me to purchase their wares.

'Buy a ballot, mister,' they normally snarl.

I generally reply in like manner.

'What for?' I'll ask.

Ballot sellers of the doorstep variety don't like to waste time or words explaining their purpose, assuming they have one. The reply is usually cryptic.

'Pensioners' is a good, safe, economical reply. They are not prepared for a lengthy discussion on the subject and they don't respond kindly to cracks like 'What would I do with a pensioner if I won one?'

It's not always wise to be more specific and ask what the proceeds are in aid of. Anything that can be misunderstood will be misunderstood although the specimen reply, 'a holiday in Majorca,' may be nearer the truth than you know.

In this case the transaction didn't take place on my doorstep but in a commercial establishment of the most respectable sort.

'It's for a good cause,' the young fellow went on and proceeded to explain it in detail. I was mesmerised with the thoroughness of his explanation. The prize was a television set and he pointed out a clergyman just leaving.

'He's just bought a couple,' he added persuasively.

A tiny complication arose at this point. There was no change in the kitty, which was kept separate and distinct from the firm's own funds. There were, though, a few coins lying on the floor of the Kellymobile parked outside the premises. That is not where I normally keep my loose change, you will understand, they had simply worked their way, in the infuriating way coins have, to the top of my pocket and had fallen all over the floor as I got out of the driver's seat.

I intended to retrieve every last one of them when I got back into the car. I didn't get where I am today . . . but never mind that now.

Impressed by the vendor's dedication to his good cause I went out at once to retrieve the price of a few ballots from the floor. I don't want to labour the point but there are certain risks attached to rummaging under the driving seat of a car. To do it effectively the rummager needs to be at least partially outside the car. This is not to be undertaken lightly on a busy main road. Projecting parts of the anatomy, a foot or a leg, for example, could easily be lopped off by a passing bus or lorry. This could make the recovery of small items of lost property less than cost-effective.

I decided to approach the problem from the opposite direction and search for the money from the passenger side. The operation was a complete success. I recovered the lot. The thing was, I'd never made my exit from my car backwards and on hands and knees from the wrong side before. Which, I imagine, was why, when I slammed the door shut, my fingers were still on the pillar.

The next few moments were interesting. Not simply for the number of bad words I dredged up effortlessly from the recesses of my vocabulary. It was the imaginative and creative way in which I combined them into new maledictions on good causes and their supporters, on ballot-sellers, the motor industry and Uncle Tom Cobley and all that must have been a source of inspiration to many passersby. It's a pity, in a way, that the clergyman had left too soon. I could have provided him with a lot of material for a long time if he'd only timed his exit right.

I was very relieved to discover, when I opened the door, that my fingers were still attached to me. Even so I bought numbers 38 and 39 with a marked lack of enthusiasm. The boss of the firm happened along in time to hear the tale of woe.

'It's a pity it hadn't happened on the premises,' he said, 'you could have got damages.'

'I've got damages,' I said huffily and held up the two fingers in an unconscious Churchillian gesture. 'Look, two of them.'

When I got home a tiler had arrived to do some long overdue repairs to the kitchen. He watched with wordless interest as I took ice cubes from the fridge, wrapped them in a tissue and applied them to the affected parts. I thought some explanation was called for. He said not a word until I was finished.

'See good causes?' he said. 'No good to anybody.'

He went back to his tiling.

If there are any advantages to trapping your fingers in a door, one of them must be that few people ever ask you what happened. Nearly everybody knows how it happened. It's already happened to them. Or they did it to somebody else. Accidentally, of course, it's not in good taste otherwise. Then there's a fortunate few, if you could so describe them, who have had it done to them. They have a psychological advantage. They have somebody to blame. That's a comfort denied to the rest of us.

By contrast, a man with personal experience told me, nobody ever enquires into the cause of a black eye. When he got his blackened orb, people gave him a wide berth. They assumed him to be of a thrawn and belligerent disposition. The clear evidence that he had been on the receiving, rather than giving, end somehow didn't seem to make its point. He enjoyed the notoriety while it lasted. He had really got his injury from that old standby of all who sport black eyes, a cupboard door. But then he' s so accident-prone about the house that there's a theory he's trying to commit suicide by instalments.

During the whole time I sported the blackened finger-tips only one individual asked for the gory details.

'What happened?' he asked, 'did you hit the wrong nails with your wee hammer?'

I knew at once that he wasn't a genuine enquirer, merely someone who had stored that wisecrack for years without a chance to use it.

'Have a bit of respect,' I told him. 'That's a new nail polish I'm road-testing for a famous cosmetics company. I can't divulge their name at this point but they're paying serious money.'

'If there's one thing I can't stand,' he growled, 'it's a smart alec.'

Alec isn't the word he used. It was another, shorter one, beginning with 'a' but you can work that out for yourself.

And just for the record, I never heard another thing about numbers 38 and 39.

27 *Behind Closed Doors*

One of my acquaintances was going into a downtown store when he noticed a lady approaching, so he held the door open for her. She spoke civilly to him and he responded in like manner, but just as he was about to let go of the door, a large percentage of the population of Belfast appeared from nowhere and began to stream into the store.

They were all disabled, apparently, or at any rate unable to get their hands out of their pockets and operate the door for themselves. He got fed up with the status of doorman very soon and seizing the chance offered by a slackening in the pedestrian flow he simply let go of the handle and went on in.

Part of his annoyance was due to the fact that out of the entire procession of shoppers, only two managed to ground out a lacklustre thank you for his courtesy. He thought that was a fairly poor return.

He should have taken a last look around before going on about his business, because he had hardly taken half a dozen steps into the store when he was seized by the shoulder, spun round and brought face to face with an angry female of very substantial proportions,

She told him he was the worst doorman she had ever met. He was rude – a remarkably unjust accusation, this – he was inefficient, which was an even less merited comment, and he was sloppy, which may or may not have been true but was his own business.

On top of all this he was a disgrace to the store. However, all these situations were about to be rectified, she assured him, for his days as a doorman were numbered. She was, she asserted, a personal friend of the manager – outraged persons are quick to claim powerful connections – and he would hear forthwith of this affront to her dignity. And she stormed off to secure his dismissal.

All of which was hard on a man who had just gone into the place to buy a pair of socks.

There is something about doors that brings out the worst in people. It's not that the technology of doors is all that complex. Our caveman ancestors mastered the more difficult undertakings, like fire and the wheel, but they wisely left the door alone. Of course, they hadn't all that much call for doors, since they had a lively fear of the dark and didn't venture out of the range of the firelight after sunset. There wasn't a lot of burglary in those happy, distant days. Anybody bold enough to make an uninvited entry during the day was sure to earn a thud on the head from the lord and master's club, on the perfectly reasonable assumption that the intruder was after either the furs or the womenfolk and not necessarily in that order.

You can tell a lot about people by the way they deal with doors. Some people, for example, are totally incapable of closing a door. They manage to get it open all right, but accustomed as they are to having underlings to do that sort of thing, they leave it lying open behind them. There is something about that which suggests a longing for the days when there were twenty shillings in the pound and every man could whip his own slaves.

There are some who are prostrated by the PUSH or PULL signs on doors. If it says Pull they push. They push hard, they sweat with exertion, they mutter about it being locked and they suffer grave injury when a literate citizen, correctly interpreting the Push sign, approaches from the other side. And who has not heard of the unfortunate who approached a glass door and didn't know it was there?

I have had mixed feelings about doors myself from the day I heard a Bible scholar expound on the statement that it is easier for a camel to pass through the eye of a needle than for a rich man to get into heaven. There was, I felt, some consolation in that for the man who discovers every Saturday night that he hasn't won the pools once again.

This scholarly chap explained that the phrase was really some kind of Middle Eastern colloquialism, that the needle referred to was a high pointed door in a city wall and the eye referred to was a smaller door set into the larger one to allow pedestrians to come and go.

Difficult, you see, but not impossible for the camel to get in, especially if you were in a small way of business and only had small camels. I'm no longer prejudiced against people who say they've been rich and they've been poor but rich is better. I just wish they'd stop jumping the queue.

Doors in buildings are not the only problem, since most cars have them too. I say most, because I often see cars about with the doors removed. There are probably sound reasons for this, like enabling the occupants to make a speedy exit if cornered by the constabulary. Generally speaking, however, it's the vehicles with doors that cause the most problems. There's the driver, for example, who believes that he's the planet's sole inhabitant and flings his door open in time to cripple a passing cyclist, and there's the passenger who does the same to some harmless being on the pavement. Let us not forget, either, the kamikaze passengers who leap on the side next the traffic and find themselves eyeball to eyeball with the radiator of a bus, sometimes from underneath.

There was a lad at school with me who never quite mastered the door. Once in a while he would get it nearly right, but nearly wasn't enough and it would drift open again. Virtually every classroom in the place opened straight into the grounds and there was a wind off the river like a knife, so that he was followed everywhere with a chorus of 'Shut that door.' Sometimes he didn't even bother to try and on one famous occasion he fell foul of a teacher who was a legend for strict discipline.

'Were you born in a field?' roared the teacher.

'No,' replied Peter, conscious of his growing reputation for living dangerously, 'I was born in a palace with swinging doors.'

Nobody spoke back to a teacher, least of all this one, in those days and Peter paid dearly for his moment of glory. He was not the only one to fall foul of authority in that school over a door. A member of staff, a somewhat eccentric cleric, was visited in his classroom one day by the headmaster, also a clergyman. Their interview wasn't too friendly, it would appear, for when the boss left the room he didn't close the door and the teacher called him back.

'I don't care if you are the headmaster,' he is alleged to have said, 'close that door.'

The head did so. He became a bishop shortly afterwards and the teacher became a curate. I'm not suggesting that there was any connection between the two things. Perish the thought. Still . . .

It's not for nothing that there's a flourishing market for spring-loaded devices for closing doors these days. They're not foolproof, of course. Some operate lazily and some would bite the leg off you. To get round this possibly lethal phenomenon, some stores use doors operated by the pressure mat method. Infallible, you would think. Not so. I once saw a busy supermarket's exits brought to a standstill by two chortling imps of about seven who took turns at stamping on the mat. The doors were whizzing back and forth like the proverbial fiddler's elbow and no amount of threatening gestures from within could dislodge the young rips, who, when they were good and ready, gave everyone the fingers with both hands and sped away.

The turnstile is not the answer either, and never was, as was witnessed by a fake obituary in the long defunct and much missed *Dublin Opinion*. A citizen of Dublin was constantly confusing the entrance and exit turnstiles in a public building and one day he suffered some minor injury.

The next edition of *Dublin Opinion* carried a cartoon depicting a tombstone on which were the words:

Erected in memory of Timothy Breach,
Who always came in by Amach
And always went out by Isteach.

28 *A Hairy Tale (or, A Fable for Our Times)*

The king stood in front of the mirror and took a good, long look at himself. Not bad, he thought. Shoes polished, knife-edge crease in the trousers, everything buttoned and zipped as appropriate, no egg on the tie, shirt crisply white and no bits of sticking plaster over any shaving cuts. He rang for the butler.

'What do you want?' growled the butler. He wasn't very good at butling, being only a cattle-dealer's mate who had been recycled through a government training scheme.

'We'll have a bit more respect around here for a start,' snapped his majesty. 'Mind your manner or there'll be trouble.'

'Don't you try any of that off-with-his-head stuff with me,' said the butler. 'I've got the goods on you, buster. My solicitor has a sealed envelope with all the details. Do you remember that weekend in . . .'

'Never mind about that now,' replied the king hastily. 'How do I look?'

'All tarted up, that's how you look,' remarked the butler, sitting down and helping himself to a cigar. 'And what's that black stuff on your head?'

'That's Greasy 5000,' said the king. 'Good, isn't it?'

'You might have let the last few hairs you had die in peace,' retorted the butler. 'You know that stuff runs if it gets wet, don't you? Give me a light.'

'That's just it,' said the king. 'I thought I might stroll down as far as the castle at the cross roads. There's a fair maiden I'd like to impress a bit.'

'Stroll, is it?' the butler jeered. 'You haven't strolled the length of yourself in eleventeen years. Why don't you just send down a couple of heavies with clubs, same as you always did before?'

'This one's different,' said the king in a dreamy voice, 'Send the meteorologist to me at once.'

'Different,' snorted the butler on the way out. 'Aw, Gawd, here we go again;' and his hysterical laughter could be heard all the way down the corridor.

Within seconds the weatherman arrived. He was carrying the tools of his trade, a sachet of bat's blood, some desiccated chicken livers and a small computer.

'I want a forecast,' ordered the king, all business.

'There's a trough of low pressure coming in from the west,' said the weatherman,' but the reports from the coastal stations aren't in yet.'

'Never mind the scientific stuff,' commented the king. 'Will it rain this afternoon?'

'The next forty-eight hours will be clear. No rain,' said the weatherman. 'Definitely.'

'You're worth every penny I pay you,' the king told him gratefully. 'How much do I pay you, by the way?'

'Well, as a matter of fact, your majesty,' said the weatherman, 'you haven't paid me anything for over a year. Any chance of something on account?'

'See me tomorrow,' answered the king. 'I have to rush out now.'

The two guards loafing at the gate were interested in the stranger coming across the courtyard.

'Here's a dodgy-looking customer,' said one, 'I'll bet his pockets are full of spoons.'

'It's a bit like the Boss,' remarked the other.

'Not at all,' said the first. 'The Boss is as grey as a badger and this guy's hair is as black as the roof of hell. Anyway, he never walks anywhere.'

'Hey, you, fatso,' shouted the second one, 'What's your game?'

'I'm the head man around here,' snarled the king. 'If you use any more words like that in my sacred and anointed presence, I'll give you such a thud on the ear your head will spin for a fortnight.'

As he walked on he could hear the two of them arguing about which would have to take the blame for insulting the king.

Down the road a little way there was a man breaking stones. There always is in stories like this.

'Good afternoon,' my good fellow,' said the king.

The stonebreaker, who was nobody's good fellow, spat and said nothing.

'Will the weather keep up, do you think?' asked the king.

'Listen,' said the stonebreaker, leaning on his hammer. 'I don't care a toss whether it rains or shines. If it rains, I get wet. If the sun shines, I get sunburn. But it won't rain today.'

'How do you know?' demanded the king.

'If it was going to rain, there'd be a haze on top of that mountain,' said the man. 'And I wish it would rain.'

'And, why, pray,' asked the king politely, 'do you wish for rain?'

'Because,' said the stonebreaker, 'taking everything into account, what with one thing and another and making due allowance for the unknown factor, you don't get all that many idiots stopping to talk to you about the weather on a wet day. Is that Greasy 5000 you've dyed your hair with?'

But the king was gone.

A quarter of a mile down the road he met a man riding a jackass. 'It's a fine day,' the king cordially greeted him.

'Not for long,' said the rider, looking at the top of the royal head with keen interest. 'I see you've been using Greasy 5000. It runs if it gets wet, you know.'

'And will it rain, do you think?' asked the king anxiously.

'Definitely,' said the rider. 'See the ears of the jackass, one pointing forward and one pointing back? A sure sign of rain, that. Never fails. If you live about here you should make for home before that stuff runs down your face.'

His royal corpulence turned and trotted for home, forgetting all about the fair maiden. He had hardly closed the front door when the rain came hissing down. He rang for the butler.

'What do you want this time?' demanded the butler crossly.

'Tell that weatherman to get himself in here sharpish,' ordered the king.

The meteorologist was there in a trice or maybe even less. Who really knows. The king handed him an envelope.

'That's a week's pay in lieu of notice,' said the king. 'You have our royal leave to push off.'

The weatherman tore open the envelope.

'It's empty,' he howled.

'Just like your prophecies,' snarled the king grimly. 'Be off or I'll have your head.'

The redundant weatherman trudged off despondently and the king rang once again for the butler.

'Listen,' complained the butler. 'I'm just about sick of this. I'm run off my feet. That's three times I've been in here this day. Do you think I've nothing better to do around this madhouse than jump every time you ring that bell? What do you want anyway?'

'I want you to get your raincoat and your umbrella and get down the road to that farmer who lives just past where the stonebreaker is working. I want you to buy his jackass. No matter what he wants, pay it. Just get the animal. All right?' said his majesty.

'You'll be well suited, the pair of you, will there be anything else?' the butler enquired.

'As a matter of fact there is,' said the king. 'You might send a couple of heavies down with clubs to invite the fair maiden up for tea.'

'That's my boy,' the butler approved and off he went whistling happily.

Thus it came to pass that the staff of the royal residence soon got used to the sight of the jackass reclining in state among bales of hay in the weatherman's office, idly flicking through the

Investor's Chronicle and adjusting his ears as impending weather conditions demanded.

And that is the real story of how the tradition of having jackasses in high government office began.